I0603857

The Tethering

A Portent of Crows

by
Evelyn Klebert

Dedication

For My Husband and My

Two Sons, The Expert Navigators of Great Change

Table of Contents

The Tethering

A Portent of Crows

Deborah Brandt

Chapter One

"Your Aunt was pretty reclusive."

"She seemed like a free spirit."

"She was extremely old-fashioned."

"I don't remember – did I meet her?"

"Debby, why don't you sell that old house? You could put a down payment on a condo."

Her Aunt Genevieve, Gena, didn't want a funeral, just a cremation and an inscription adding her name to an old family plot in Greenwood Cemetery.

"It doesn't really matter much to me. There is a little money set aside for the expense as far as the remains, but quite honestly, it won't have anything to do with me at that point."

Her aunt was pragmatic. Her aunt was eccentric. Her aunt was a thousand things that didn't necessarily coalesce comfortably together.

"The house is paid for." Her mother had looked a bit displeased at the recognition that her advice had simply been brushed aside so cavalierly. She showed up two days after Aunt Gena's passing. Her other aunt, a designation she used loosely — Lila, Delilah — hadn't even bothered. Genevieve was the youngest of the three girls, just 54 when she died.

"Yes, but there are expenses."

"I'll manage," her voice, feeling a bit strained and drowned out in the rage of commentary. Her mother's presence was irritating, given her lack of presence at pretty much every other time. To say the least, they weren't close. Margaret had her new family, a remarriage after Deborah's father had vanished into parts unknown when Deborah was a teenager, and then Deborah had spent the last three and a half years living with her aunt — the last six months as a caregiver of sorts, once her heart unexpectedly and relentlessly began to fail.

"There's nothing to be upset about in death. This is part of life. A change, that's all."

A change, yes, her aunt had been correct. But for her, an insidious one, not a calamitous change she'd braced herself for but instead just quiet. Quiet couched in the thousand little daily reminders of what life had been like when her aunt was with her, at least in the flesh.

"So, I want you to be ready."

"Ready? For what?" She'd questioned.

"When things change for you, Deb — you're not like everyone else, you know."

That was the litany Aunt Gena promoted, sweet Aunt Gena, always kind, always nurturing in a way her self-absorbed mother had consistently failed to be. Yes, in a way, Deborah believed there was a morsel of truth in what her aunt had said, but not at all in the kindly and, she suspected, indulgent way that she intended. No, instead, Deborah had always felt out of step, in fact somewhat alien and different than everyone around her — a reality she'd tried to submerge, even from herself.

"Are you going to get another place?"

"Are you going to get a roommate?" The cacophony of advice prettily disguised as questions felt deafening at times — friends or rather acquaintance friends in college piling on the stack of commentary. She was struggling to finish her bachelor's degree in journalism with a minor in history, not precisely pragmatic in the world view of things, but then she never claimed to be.

"No, not now," she'd answered. She didn't want to begin to contemplate a future without Aunt Gena. That lovely, intuitive lady had filled a void in her life that she'd had no idea existed until she came to live with her. If you've lived all your life without a coat and suddenly got one, did you ever really acknowledge that you needed it before? Probably, though maybe that wasn't the best analogy. But if she was using it, Aunt Gena, metaphorically, had been her coat, a coat that she sorely missed with a tangible ache. Without her, the world felt so bitter and chilled now.

How she missed her and how she tried to clamp down on that reality by keeping things unchanged — the house, her routine. The only difference, and such a monumental difference, was that she was doing everything alone.

Her neck felt irritated, stinging really.

"It hasn't been seen, you know, for generations," Aunt Gena had observed.

Of course, she remembered, then she'd laughed, not taking it seriously. Admittedly, there was a common consensus, heavily influenced by her mother, that Aunt Gena was more than a bit out there. But Deborah didn't mind and wasn't entirely sure this was true — and wasn't convinced that it even mattered. So, she congenially played along. "Wow, no kidding. Do you have it?"

"No, but I have watched for it. I knew someone would one day, someone significant."

Often conversations veered off like this. She refused to analyze too deeply why her aunt said or believed the fanciful things she did. It just seemed to be a part of who she was.

Deborah rubbed the spot on the side of her neck, a curious birthmark, a half-circle sort of scar-looking thing situated on her skin somewhere near her collarbone. *"What does it mean?"* she'd prodded because she liked to hear her talk, and in truth, she was curious.

"It means you're different Deb."

And she'd smiled and nodded. That wasn't such a terrible thing, even if it wasn't true, to be special in some way, not terrible at all.

"Why don't you?"

"What?" she looked up with distraction.

"Ross, why don't you start seeing him?"

"What? I am. I mean we see each other sometimes," feigning ignorance while being completely cognizant of what was being asked. It was a dodging technique, one that seldom worked, she did recognize upon reflection.

Her arm's length friend frowned at her. "No, I mean boyfriend, girlfriend type seeing. He likes you."

Deborah smiled, slowly pulling off her reading glasses to give her time to consider an acceptable response. She did reflect on the fact that she was only twenty-five and should not have to wear reading glasses, but the print in some of these volumes was so small that she couldn't imagine any normal healthy eye being able to read it. So, reassuring herself, she didn't feel so decrepit. "Look, Jessica, that's nice of you to suggest, but I am busy, trying to finish a degree, and working at the art gallery. And the bottom line is I don't have time for much social stuff."

Jessica was a bit younger, at least several years, luminescent with her light brown skin and curly dark hair, more enthusiastic, and much more of an extrovert than Deborah could imagine ever being. In fact, Jessica arrived just short of being bubbly. In a nutshell, she was the antithesis of everything she believed herself to be. She grimaced, flipping through her dusty volume. It was ridiculous. By all rights, this stuff should be on computer now. "Don't have time. Is that really true Deborah?"

"Of course, it is. What else would it be?"

She shrugged. Jessica was probably as close to a "real friend" as she'd ever had, though admittedly, she still held her a bit at a distance, somewhat inexplicably, perhaps. It was just her way. "I don't know, just wondering if you might be keeping something from me."

"Keeping what?" she muttered, trying to focus again on the almost archaically written text in front of her. It was for a research paper in Early European history, and the teacher wanted them to peruse actual volumes, not just virtual ones.

"Maybe you just don't like boys at all. Maybe you're—"

"No," Now that did refocus her attention. "I'm busy and not interested in dating. That's it. Believe me."

Again, an exaggerated shaking of her head, "I just don't get you. He's cute."

"Of course he is. He's just not right for me."

The city of New Orleans in October was hot and muggy generally. And it felt as though it clung to her skin like a film. Deborah Brandt lived alone in the house near the corner of Banks and S. Alexander Streets. It was an older, wood-framed, cozy sort of bungalow style where she'd resided with her Aunt Gena until last spring. With some money left by her aunt, a college fund set up by her absent father, and her salary from a part-time job as a receptionist in the Sauveterre Art Gallery, Deborah continued to make ends meet — somewhat strenuously, sometimes perilously, but as best as she could. There was family, other family spread across the country, primarily her mom up in North Carolina with her new siblings, a half-sister, and half-brother. But none of them had ever been close to her, not as her aunt had. Sadly, and undeniably, she felt as though now she was all alone in the world.

As she sat reading a textbook on cyber journalism, there was a familiar stinging around her neck area. Walking over to a cherry wood, oval wall mirror situated just in the front foyer of the house, she pulled the collar of her cotton t-shirt down and exposed her neck. The half-circle birthmark looked aggravated tonight. In fact, it was fire engine red. She brushed her reddish-brown shoulder-length hair behind her ears to look closer.

It wasn't terribly large, about the size of a dime. Usually, it faded into the tone of her skin, except for a few raised ridges, but tonight it seemed absolutely aggravated.

"It's the sign, you know."

She frowned at the recollection. Her aunt had first noticed the birthmark on a day several years ago when Deborah was helping her buff up the shiny wooden floors in the main bedroom. It was well before Aunt Gena had gotten sick.

"What does that mean — the sign?" she murmured, not wholly connecting with whatever her aunt was going on about at the moment.

Aunt Gena was tall and thin, wiry in some respects, with dark brown hair lightly sprinkled with gray, not nearly as reddish as hers. She remembered she'd frowned at Deborah a bit. "Didn't your mother tell you anything?" It was no well-kept secret that there was more than a bit of bad blood between the Brevard sisters. To say they were not close was more than an understatement. It was more accurate to say that each, in their way, had inexplicably amputated their siblings from their lives. In truth, the fact that Deborah was able to salvage a relationship with her Aunt Gena was rather remarkable.

"No, actually, I don't ever remember her mentioning a sign," she said, looking back at her a bit bemused. She loved her aunt dearly and enjoyed listening to her eccentric ramblings.

Aunt Gena, undaunted and not seeming to acknowledge Deborah's skepticism, continued, "Well, let's just say that from time to time, it appears amongst the women in the Gauthier bloodline."

Gauthier, she recalled, was an old family name on her mother's side. That much she was vaguely aware of. "The sign? Oh, you mean this birthmark on my neck. Well, it is a bit odd, isn't it?" She didn't mind indulging her. She liked her stories and found the gentle lilt of her speaking voice soothing to her often-aggravated nerves. Yes, Deborah did admit her emotions were always on the edgy side of the spectrum.

Aunt Gena went on, "My mother told me about it a long time ago, to watch for it, said that it was a special designation."

She waited for elaboration, then coaxed. Aunt Gena was fond of dramatic pauses. But then again, Deborah suspected they were just to ascertain if she was really being listened to. "Designation for what exactly?"

"For the paladin."

"Paladin?" she repeated slowly, now looking at her aunt with genuine confusion. "Sounds suspiciously like something out of Dungeons and Dragons."

And at that moment, Deborah had caught something unexpected in her aunt's eyes, something entirely unexpected, almost a sadness. "Well, it means, my dear, that you might be forced to live your life a bit differently."

The birthmark continued to sting. Deborah couldn't remember it being so painful before. Although there had been times she had felt it inflamed on her neck, burning like some sort of strange brand. When Aunt Gena had passed away earlier in the year, she'd felt it acutely but differently, like a tingling awareness. But tonight, it was simply unbearably aggravating. She could, of course, get it looked at by a dermatologist but dismissed that option rather quickly. What would they know of sacred family lineage and profound birthmarks that signaled one's destiny? This she thought with amusement and fond recollections of her aunt.

She glanced up at Aunt Gena's cuckoo clock over the mantle that would be doing its manic dance at any moment, nearly seven in the evening. She had no business contemplating this with the amount of schoolwork she had facing her, but her skin was crawling. There was no question, at least in her mind, that she had to get out. Grabbing her purse, she headed out of the house to a small coffee shop down Banks Street.

Unsettled, unsettled everywhere, on her skin, in the pit of her stomach, in her very thoughts, nothing seemed to be appeasing this pervasive impression tonight. She sipped the unsatisfying coffee, wishing dearly she'd gotten something a little less bitter. She was tired and needed a sugary energy, not this morose concoction with its dark chocolate mixed in. Most nights, this would work for her. After all, she didn't have a sweet tooth, but not tonight. Yes, unsettled was the word, though actually bordering on anxious. And the harsh taste was hitting her stomach in a nauseating fashion.

The Coffee Stop, a little hole-in-the-wall establishment on the edge of Banks and Joliet that she frequented, was largely empty tonight. Not so surprising, Tuesday evenings didn't seem to warrant a crowd. There was one couple toward the back seated on a leather sofa across from a fireplace that she had never actually seen lit. Other than them, there was a girl, a little younger than her she thought, spread out on one of the tables with a laptop and notebooks.

Enviously, she regretted not bringing some of her work with her. It was certainly quiet enough for it, and again she acknowledged with guilt that she had no business being out with the pile of work facing her back at the house. Her schedule made it so easy to fall behind, particularly since Aunt Gena had passed away. The stress and emotion of that time had taken a huge chunk of energy and robbed her of motivation that she had yet to recapture. She took another sip of the bitter coffee, more than anything, because she didn't want to waste the four dollars she'd spent on it.

"Well, you know, it might not happen for you."

She'd grimaced at her Aunt Gena's comment. Being indulgent only spread so far, and now, looking back at that relatively obscure moment, she recalled her tolerance feeling uncharacteristically paper thin. "What might not happen exactly?"

"You might never be called into service."

"Service?" she stopped peeling potatoes. Her aunt had opted to make a huge pot of vegetable soup as the weather had just begun to turn cold. And, of course, Deborah was drafted, or rather pulled away from battling through a school paper, to help. It wasn't as though she minded. Usually, she liked these little chats they'd have in her aunt's kitchen, but the timing was more than a bit inconvenient. "What exactly does that mean, service?" she asked a bit too tersely.

"I know this is confusing, my dear, given your modern sensibilities, but our bloodline means that we come from an old family from which some are called to serve mankind in times of difficulty."

Her breath escaped in nearly a hiss. Her mother had cautioned her on more than one occasion that Aunt Gena wasn't operating with a full deck. And at this aggravating moment, she'd hoped dearly that she hadn't jumped from harmless eccentricity into some sort of odd senility. "I really don't—"

"No, I can see clearly, dear, that you don't understand. But you need to stop thinking and listen a bit. If there comes a time when you are needed, you will be contacted by someone, your counterpart, I suppose."

"My, what exactly?"

Her aunt seemed to hesitate. "Someone who will help you understand your special gifts, someone who will help you and," and then she'd hesitated oddly, "be a powerful match for you."

"Match, what do you mean by match?" she snapped a bit too sternly.

It had been strange as she remembered it now. In fact, looking back, it had almost seemed that her aunt was downright flustered by her direct questioning. "What I mean to say is that there is one person in the world who you may or may not meet, who is the only one suited to you," then she'd paused, choosing her words carefully, "as a mate."

It was a bit comical in retrospect, though of course, not at the time. Back then, she had been a bit shocked and flustered that her sweet aunt had even used that oddly archaic-sounding word — mate. "I — I have no clue what you mean Aunt Gena."

"I mean that if you ever take another as your lover, it will be disastrous."

Disastrous was indeed the word she'd used. Absolutely ridiculous, and naturally, she'd pushed it aside, deciding that her aunt's heart condition wasn't allowing enough oxygen to circulate to her brain. These odd lapses should no doubt be expected.

And it wasn't a matter they'd discussed much further. Her aunt's condition worsened, and Deborah's energy became focused on caring for her. Though there was that one time she had asked a particular question toward the end "Why did you never marry Aunt Gena?"

And she remembered her aunt had smiled at her a bit sadly at the question. "Well, it wasn't my fate to find the one who was right for me. Everyone, with or without your special birthmark, has suitors more suitable to them spiritually. And if you don't have the good fortune to find them, sometimes it's best not to embroil yourself with one who would only complicate your existence. Of course, one must make allowances for spiritual paths. But I have no regrets. My life has been full."

She shook her head, her mind overwhelmed with confusion at her aunt's rambling. "I just don't understand this. This is not the way the world works."

She grimaced, and Deborah knew she was in pain. She'd deteriorated so much from the protracted illness. She had no business peppering her with personal questions at this point. "Most people never understand how the world truly works, my dear. But suffice to say that we are different. We can't afford the cost of erring in this regard. Be careful, my dear. Not to be too Victorian, guard your virtue, and be awake and aware."

She felt a tangible chill pass through her, and she wondered, for not the first time that evening, if she'd been foolish to come out tonight. Her skin felt uncomfortable, as though a thick layer of irritation was on her. "Be aware of energy shifts, Deborah. Sometimes it is the only warning you may have of impending peril." Aunt Gena had coached her on this during one of her more lucid moments. There had always been an odd dichotomy in their relationship. Deborah's mind had told her emphatically to be dismissive, but on a level, she had soaked it in. Everything that lovely, delicate woman had told her, she had soaked in and tucked away.

She took a quick last sip of the bitter coffee she'd ordered and stood up. Eyes, eyes were on her. She could feel them distinctly on her back. It was one of them, one of those people in the coffee shop, but she couldn't tell exactly who. With quiet determination, she walked outside. The coolness of the night air unexpectedly hit her squarely in the face. So strange, it hadn't been very long that she'd been out, but the temperature had dropped perceptively. Turning the corner at Banks St., she started to walk home quickly without looking back.

Deborah closed the door and locked it behind her. Her head ached, and oddly it felt as though she was trembling all over. Going out tonight had been a bad idea. She felt tangibly worse than she had before.

Moving upstairs, she lit a candle next to her bed before she grabbed some nightclothes and headed into the shower. Water, washing off, was a simple cure that her aunt had coached. When one encounters bad energy, drown it in water, and wash your old clothing so as not to re-infect.

As the shower's warm water began to hit her skin, she began to feel some relief. But she also felt drained, exhausted. *"You have to be careful to protect your energy, always."*

Sometimes she wished she could simply disregard all the strangeness that Aunt Gena had tried to impart to her. But then, that had been a large part of who Aunt Gena had been, and she didn't want to forget, not even a scrap of her. So, all the advice, the peculiar way Aunt Gena looked at the world, it was still with Deborah. She carried it and would simply have to make peace with that reality as her aunt's words continued to reverberate around her head. Though at times, she did just yearn for an ordinary life.

Then again, Aunt Gena had often repeated that there was no such thing. It may appear so on the surface, but truly, it's never the case. No one lives a life without complications.

And undeniably, on top of everything, there were the dreams, dreams that were so real and tangible and yet profoundly impossible — disconcerting, to say the least. They had plagued her, increasingly since her aunt had passed away. This night, after the debacle at the coffee shop, she moved restlessly through the house. Her feet were bare, and she wore only a long white t-shirt that ended around mid-thigh. Although on warm summer nights, this might very well be her attire, though this night was not warm. In fact, as she crept around the darkened twists and turns of her aunt's former abode, she was quite chilled, all of her — her skin, her blood, her very bones. And as her feet hit the floor, they chafed and hurt as though the wooden floors were now rough and abrasive, not smoothly polished as she still kept them. As nonsensical as this contrast seemed, the sharp biting pains in her feet attested to the concreteness of the dream.

"It's not real, you know, not exactly — more figurative."

She heard the commentary spoken, though not exactly. "What does that mean?"

"By figurative, I mean more representative of energy than your reality."

"My reality?" she questioned as she carefully curved around the small wooden staircase in Aunt Gena's house.

"What you see with your eyes."

"I still don't—"

"Come downstairs. I'll attempt to explain."

A disconnected voice or something of the like speaking to her in her mind. This was what she was freely following instructions from. Surely not prudent, but then again this was ostensibly *"a dream."*

She reached the landing, again her feet feeling brush burned. Was it really so bad here? She'd attempted to keep the place up since her aunt had passed.

"It's negative energy from the area, nothing to do with cleanliness."

The den downstairs was dark, though the shutters on the long front windows fluttered as though they'd been knocked open by a breeze or some sort of — "

"Storm," the thought was completed rather abruptly.

The shadows flickered jarringly in the room, no doubt because of all the open windows. The lightest sprays of rain bristled through the air that she breathed.

She focused on whoever it was, sitting in her aunt's rocking chair near the fireplace, a fireplace whose embers were almost extinguished but not quite. There was still the briefest of flickering light in there.

"Should I be concerned that there is a stranger in my house?" she said much too calmly for the circumstances she found herself in, but then again, normal standards felt quite out the window at present.

"Ownership is a faulty construct. None of us truly owns anything."

She leaned back against the short maple post of the staircase railing. "You're not really lecturing me, are you, whatever you are?"

She saw a shift in the shadows but not much. But the storm outside—

"It's figurative like I said. Things around here are getting difficult."

"Why?" she murmured, but she felt a weakness, as though a great puff of energy had been expelled right out of her chest.

"Things come in cycles, and they are trying to make their move now."

"They?" she repeated, thinking for perhaps the first time of the texture of the voice she heard, deep, rich, but also gravelly. Familiar? Not exactly, but the tone undeniably resonated with her.

"The low ones, they're trying to make inroads. This area is a significant energy point. It has to be protected."

"Protected?" she whispered. She saw or did she feel the shadowed figure rise from the chair, and it seemed suddenly as though her knees would give way. What was it? Recognition? Power? Understanding felt just beyond her reach.

"You're so weak," it whispered all around her.

She breathed in deeply and felt herself falling but also felt arms, human arms, wrapping around her. "I know," she answered, though it didn't feel exactly like her.

But then there were hands on her, energizing her, awakening her, hands that felt familiar from a different time, a different place. "Who are you?" she rasped.

"Soon," was the answer.

The Counterpart

Chapter Two

How could he explain the true nature of the world to those who chose to embrace the illusion of what they believed? Frankly, it was impossible until they were drowning in the truth and had no choice but to acknowledge it or go under.

The night before had been an exceedingly difficult evening. For him, it was most obvious as to why. To others, they would simply feel inexplicably irritable, or perhaps more — angry, enraged, depressed, depending on the malleability of the individual. The truth was the energy was turbulent, heavy, and, yes, unequivocally negative. For him, it was as tangible as walking through a heavy fog filled with toxic chemicals. It was a night to stay home and allow the cloud of bad energy pass as one would shelter from a sudden thunderstorm, but unfortunately, it seemed that she had made another choice.

It had been just three years now that he'd lived in the city. At the onset, it was quite clear that this area would be a place of great spiritual activity, both good and bad. And more than a decade before, he'd first been told about her, told that once they met, finally connected, things would become much clearer. And also, regrettably, they would draw attention. That was the nature of power. Of course, given all of this, it was primary that the time be right to make contact, not too early and as well, not too late.

These thoughts plagued him as he waited, albeit not always patiently. And it was clear to him, as clear as anything, that this night, this particularly difficult night was not the right time. However, all of this didn't change the fact that she was potentially in great peril. And it frustrated him to no end that she would willfully be out on a night like this, and how extraordinarily unprotected she was allowing herself to be.

He'd parked his black sedan on one of the side streets adjacent to Banks. He was familiar with the neighborhood, although he did not frequent it. Being in the area too often, he believed, might just tip his hand before he was ready. At this point, with keeping himself at such a distance, it was difficult to gauge how sensitive she was.

The light was waning yet had not entirely disappeared. As he slowly walked along Olympia St. heading to Banks, he was alerted by an odd rustling in the trees he was passing. What he could clearly see in the dimming light was far too many crows filling the somewhat barren branches. He took a sharp breath inward. It wasn't precisely that he believed in superstitious omens but rather understood that animals, like people, were affected by shifts in energy. In fact, one might say that they were more attuned than people who cluttered their minds with unimportant incidentals and distractions.

Throughout his life, he had spent an inordinate amount of time arduously training and learning to reign in and monitor his mental faculties. With this, he could be more aware and responsive to the spiritual shifts in the natural world.

And there was undeniably one taking place this evening, one that had alerted this particular species of bird.

"Blackbirds, especially crows, and ravens, collect when there is a concentration of energy."

"Energy, what sort of energy?"

His Uncle Silas had furrowed his tawny brow, or rather he had in his recollection. "Negative usually, I'm afraid. I know these birds get a bad rap, but in this instance, it is true. They herald a great concentration of negativity, act as a marker and perhaps as a buffer."

Throughout his life, his Uncle Silas had often served as a mentor and guide in these matters. The truth was that he grew up differently than most, although he knew without question that he wasn't alone in this regard. For him, the unseen was commonplace. What others might disregard as fantasy was accepted as normal as learning to ride a bike, as one's first steps or words. The shock of it was that everyone didn't live the same way or acknowledge truths that were as basic as drawing breath.

So, as a result, at a relatively young age, at least the age of reasoning, he'd also learned discretion and secrecy. In effect, he would always be two people, one that the world would know and another — his true self that only the like-minded would be aware of.

"You need to make some sort of contact with your counterpart."

His uncle was a warm, large-frame fellow, hair slightly graying with an overly proportioned mustache and a small goatee. Uncle Silas, Silas Bayle, had ostensibly been the only parent he'd known since his ninth year. His father had not been in the picture, ostensibly abandoning his young family early on, and his mother had completely transferred custody to her brother when he was young.

But of course, he'd always known Uncle Silas. Ever since he could remember, he was a part of his world growing up as his mother retreated increasingly into a personal world of isolation.

"What's the matter with her?" he remembered asking the only stable presence he'd ever truly known.

"It's complicated, my boy. She's extremely sensitive to, well, almost everything, and living as we do, in a physical shell, is simply becoming more and more painful to her."

He didn't understand, and yet he did. You see, his mother had always spoken to him more from other planes than the one where their physical selves existed. "I'm sorry, my little one. My path is drawing me away from you, but I will always be with you, just perhaps not at all in the way you expect."

It upset him, but he accepted. He'd learned even at that tender age that one should not impose your expectations upon life but rather be in accordance with what is, what is true. After a while, she stopped speaking entirely. That was when Uncle Silas moved in with them, into that white frame house just on the border of the Ozark mountains in Missouri. He knew his uncle was a traveler and that, somehow, his business drew him to many diverse locations throughout the world. But that year, that last year, he stayed with them.

"My boy, it's important you be strong. Your mother is moving to another place, a place where she can exist comfortably."

"Do you mean a hospital, Uncle Silas?"

And then his uncle looked at him oddly as though what he'd said was nonsensical. "No, no, my boy, she isn't ill. She is simply evolving. She's going to a special place where people operating on the same plane as her live. It's not a bad thing at all. Her only concern is you. All else would be joy for her, except the thought of leaving you, leaving you physically. You'll see. She will always be with you, guiding you, visiting with you, helping you, but it will be different."

"But where will I go?"

And then the older man had smiled broadly. "I hope you will stay with me. I will oversee your education and hopefully be a friend to you."

He'd nodded, feeling confused because, after all, he was just nine. "All right," he'd whispered.

"Please don't be sad, my boy. I promise you that your life will be a wonder."

He studied his surroundings intently. The light of the day had dissipated completely, but the streetlamps on Banks more than illuminated the area. On both sides of the street, there was a profuse gathering of the crows, silent but continuing to fill the branches like ebony ornaments. Silent, yes, but undeniably not at peace, restless, anxious, agitated — he could feel this acutely emanating from them.

Why hadn't she stayed in tonight? It was a terrible time to be out. He opened his awareness as far as he dared. He didn't want to make himself vulnerable, yet he knew he must find her.

And then, he could feel her moving again. The birds had thinned as he approached the coffee shop where she'd entered moments before. But there were still some, some perched on the rooftops in the area, waiting and watching, it seemed.

No, he hesitated as he saw one zoom down fluidly into the middle of the road. He was wrong. They were searching. He pulled the collar of his jacket up a bit more and continued to walk right past the coffee house.

Crossing the street, he waited as inconspicuously as he could manage. He had no idea where this would end tonight, but he needed to see that she was safe.

As he stood outside the establishment, he focused intently on investigating within. Allowing his awareness to expand slowly, definitively, inside the coffee house, he breathed deeply as the inner vision took over. She was sitting alone at a small round dark wooded table just past the counter near the left wall of the shop. Following the vibrations beyond her, there was a young couple seated on a sofa facing an unlit fireplace and, even further to the right, a young woman with a computer and books spread out on a table. As he struggled to maintain his awareness, his head began to pound with stress and irritation. Something was off here. He encouraged his vision to shift further, allowing him to see energy auras. The woman at the table was bleeding a sort of turquoise-colored light mixed with splotches of pink, indicating extreme focus with some anxiety but nothing to be concerned with. As his focus approached the couple, he started to see something disturbing, splotches of dark colors mixed with a red glow of agitation. There was a profound instability in the pair that was deliberately exacerbated by this night's negative energy.

Emanations of fear and aggression were coming from them, which concerned him greatly. Clearly, they needed money and were sizing up both women at the coffee house as potential targets. Focusing on them intensely, he worked to plant an acute fear of being caught if they attempted anything. And just as he did, there was a responsive movement with the girl, as though she'd subconsciously picked up on his efforts.

She hurriedly collected her things as he slowly withdrew his surveillance.

As she exited the coffee shop, he distantly followed behind, monitoring her progress until she was finally back in her house again. Once she was safely inside, he slowly walked past. He was relieved that she appeared to be staying put for the evening, and the protective energy around the dwelling still seemed intact. They wouldn't find her here.

For a moment, he allowed himself to feel her inside the structure. She was bathing. It startled him at first, but then again, that made sense. The negative energy was so thick tonight, and undeniably, on some level, she knew it. And then he felt more, the shower's hot water cascading off her skin, making her drowsy.

As analytical as he aspired to be at times, he wasn't made of stone. Everything within him pushed him to go to her, let her know who he was, what they could be together. But he resisted. It wasn't time yet, but not much longer.

Late that evening, when he returned home, he decided to recheck her house just to make sure it was secure. He supposed it would have been prudent to withdraw, but he told himself he could plant impressions in her dream that might influence her, might help guide her, at the very least, to be more careful. He sunk into a deep meditation and approached it from another level of reality, one that curiously enough collided with an out of body experience that Deborah Brandt was interpreting as a dream at the same time.

These were the excuses he used, but he had to admit that he was drawn, profoundly, undeniably drawn to her. Being this close to her, he could already feel the snap of electricity between them, their thoughts and emotions. And so, he'd allowed himself indulgences, the feel of her skin beneath his hands, even in their astral states, creating energy.

Next year, he would be thirty-three. The woman, Deborah Brandt, was just twenty-five, a bit younger. He'd thought to wait a while before their official introduction, but fate seemed to have something else in mind. It was clear now that events were shifting, and agencies were on the move in the city. He'd like to believe the presence of that malevolent couple in the coffee shop was just a coincidence, but he didn't believe in coincidences. Things were escalating, and he needed her help, her abilities, her energy to meet what was coming. And without being self-deceptively arrogant on any level, he knew, without question, that she needed him as well.

Chapter Three

Deborah knew without question that she would eventually have to look for another job. The Sauveterre Art Gallery, where she worked, was on Chartres Street in the French Quarter which for anyone living in the city made parking challenging at best. Undeniably, it was best to buy some sort of long-term pass at one of the nearby lots because parking daily was astronomical, and trying to find a free space on a consistent basis was just living in a dream world. But that wasn't the reason she needed a different job.

Her boss, an elderly Italian businessman, Cesaire Segretti, who had acquired the gallery less than five years earlier from the Sauveterre family, was decent enough and more than willing to work with her class schedule. And there was another receptionist, Colleen Marsh, well into her thirties, who helped Mr. Segretti with the books and paper trail end of the business. Colleen was a tall, slim, brunette woman, angular in features and, truth be told, angular and sharp in personality as well. While she had a business-like demeanor, she was unquestionably a bit unvarnished in her people skills.

That was why she supposed Mr. Segretti kept Deborah on. He clearly liked her better for the people-oriented end of the work, and she had to admit the pay was good. But despite the affable working conditions, it was more than clear that she needed to find another job. There were other considerations, in many ways pressing considerations.

"You'll find your sensitivities growing, Deborah, as you grow closer to the time."

"What time exactly?"

But Aunt Gena had dodged the specifics of her reference. "Be aware of your feelings. They may just make things uncomfortable for you."

Of course, back then, Deborah dismissed the comment and filed it away as it seemed vague and disconnected. But the memory did float in when things began to happen, and the gallery itself or rather the objects within seemed to illustrate her aunt's reference rather concretely.

Her station was at the ornate Edwardian inlaid rosewood desk in the front foyer of the reception hall. She always made sure to dress the part for work, today in a fitted black pencil skirt, long-sleeve white and black silk blouse with a large floppy tie cascading from the neck, and the three-inch-high black pumps — any higher and she might suffer balance problems. It was an outfit she'd rarely used in her daily life but entirely necessary for this particular line of work.

Today, she'd only been at the gallery for a few moments, coming in just after lunch. She was relieving Colleen and staying until closing, which would be five. Often, a whole shift would pass with nothing much happening. It was not a particularly demanding occupation, which was why she had her laptop strategically perched on an adjacent wooden file cabinet where Colleen stashed customer information. Surreptitiously, she might get some schoolwork done or surf the internet if she was bored. The sad truth was that she was often window dressing here, which, for her purposes, wasn't a problem. At present, she didn't need a fulfilling occupation, just one to pay a few bills.

But then again, there was that other problem as of late, the fact that increasingly all she could feel here was distracted.

It had already begun almost immediately when she entered the premises, the strange prickly feeling canvassing her skin, a sort of inexplicable, unsettling irritation. "Energy, you'll become more aware of it."

She didn't really understand, except to say that her aunt had stressed that it was part of everything. Everything, including inanimate objects, held an energy, she'd explained. And evidently, the objects here, paintings, sculptures, were so old that they undoubtedly held all sorts of energy.

She glanced up from her computer screen, alerted that Mr. Segretti and someone else was approaching her desk from the direction of his office on the far side of the gallery. Quickly, she closed the laptop. She needed to appear at least that she was doing her job.

"Deborah," the portly Italian man who was her boss called as he drew nearer.

Smiling, she stood up hurriedly, straightening her well-fitted skirt and trying to appear professional. Cesaire Segretti, outfitted in one of his expensive dark suits, was well into his seventies, with a full head of gray hair and a round, ruddy, pleasing face that had zeroed directly in on her. Beside him today was a younger man, blondish, it seemed at first glance, several inches taller than her boss, dressed in a tan sports coat and dark pants. "What can I do for you, Mr. Segretti?" she asked smoothly. She never called him Cesaire, though she had heard Colleen do so often enough. As it was, he seemed more than comfortable with the professional distinction she maintained with him.

"Deborah, I'd like to introduce Mr. Wren," he spoke in a heavy Italian accent that always seemed to make his words flow together in peculiar harmony.

She nodded in Mr. Wren's direction. He appeared on the slender side and had dark eyes, or so it seemed at first glance.

Mr. Segretti continued to ramble on amiably, as was his custom. After all, at heart, Deborah had always sensed he was a salesman, yes, a seller of fine art, but a salesman, nonetheless. "Mr. Wren is interested in our collection of historic 18th and 19th-century European paintings on the third floor. I'm running a bit late for my appointment at the bank, and I'd like you to escort Mr. Wren upstairs."

She swallowed on a suddenly dry throat. Now, this was unusual. Rarely did she venture beyond chatting amiably with customers right here at this desk. The truth was that she hadn't bothered in her year of working here to learn much about the pieces in the gallery. She'd only viewed this job as an amiable stopgap until she could land a more suitable position at the University. "Of course, but perhaps Colleen."

"No, no, Colleen is tied up with a conference call, an important negotiation."

"Oh," she answered awkwardly, wondering if, indeed, that was true at all. He usually escorted serious customers about himself, not wanting Colleen to spend too much time with clients. She tended to run them off occasionally with her abrasiveness. "Of course," and then she stepped away from the desk. "Just this way, Mr. Wren," she said with as much polish as she could muster.

Deborah didn't like the third floor. For lack of a better description, it felt oddly thick to her. That was the only word she could come up with to describe it. Thick, meaning actually harder to breathe in some respects than other areas of the gallery. There was a small, cramped elevator just past Mr. Segretti's office that they traveled in to go upstairs —another space she wasn't too fond of. On their journey together, she tried not to glance at Mr. Wren too often, not wanting to be rude, but on the brief ride, she did find him remarkably quiet.

"Have you worked here long?" It was a bit jarring when he finally did speak, his voice piercing the silence.

"Just under a year, really," she responded in the pleasant, modulated tone she'd adapted for her work facade. "Mr. Segretti has acquired quite an extensive collection of European art."

"Yes, that's what he told me," he said softly. His voice was deep in some respects but smooth.

The elevator stopped, jolting ever so slightly. Silently, she drew in a deep breath as the door sluggishly eased open. This was an old building, as old as any in the French Quarter, with a relatively dated elevator that always made her nervous. But other than some steps up a dark, dank stairwell unfit for potential customers, this was the only way to the third floor. She strode out of the elevator, feigning confidence, and heard Mr. Wren move behind her, then to her side.

This first room on the third floor had a low ceiling but was long, in fact unnaturally long, taking a few bends inconsistent with its expected geometric proportions. But as a showroom, which was its function, she supposed it sufficed. Throughout were easels, golden, silver, and brass colored with heavy, ornate paintings perched atop. She couldn't help it. She shivered as they walked further within, although the temperature was quite comfortable. "All paintings are labeled, and we have detailed histories of each, their previous owner, the artists, country of origin. Mr. Segretti is quite extensive in his research." She paused as Mr. Wren walked up to her, in fact, right in front of her as she spoke, looking at her a bit oddly. Her eyes widened a bit at his proximity. "Was there something in par—"

"No," he'd cut her off in mid-sentence. Dark brown eyes, she could see them more clearly now and rather pronounced bone structure.

"I see," she murmured, not stepping back but holding her ground under his unexpected scrutiny. "Well, perhaps you'd like to just peruse the collection, and I'll wait here in case you have any questions."

"You don't seem to like this place," he commented a bit under his breath. His enunciation was somewhat clipped, but she couldn't identify a particular accent. He definitely wasn't local.

Her heart was beating slightly more strongly in response to this somewhat awkward conversation. The idle thought suddenly danced across her mind. Was she in some sort of jeopardy here? "I wouldn't say that. This room is filled with history."

And then a slight smile touched his lips. He had a full mouth, what her Aunt Gena might have termed almost sensuous lips. "That may be the problem. History, by virtue of what it is, is filled with divergences."

She straightened up a bit. He was staring directly into her eyes. Most people didn't do that, particularly not with someone they'd just met. "I'm afraid I don't follow Mr. Wren."

"Yes, well, why don't we start with you calling me Daniel."

His comment seemed to hang in the air indefinitely, for such an odd uncomfortable stretch of time. She understood of course, that it was the paintings, the sculptures, the old stuff that pressed down so heavily on her — the energies. Her aunt had explained to her, "As you grow in sensitivity, some things will become more intolerable to you. Things you might have ignored before. Now they will become a weight, something tangible to wrestle with." That was the real reason why she couldn't stay here much longer. Whether she'd ever accepted anything that her Aunt Gena had told her, she'd begrudgingly accepted this. And this was the reason that she pondered as she stared into the very dark eyes of Daniel Wren. There was light there but peculiar light, hidden light that she didn't understand. "I'm sorry. What did you say?" she whispered.

He was standing too close, too close for the truly short duration of their acquaintance. "I said I'd like you to call me Daniel."

She swallowed on a dry throat, and her voice felt somewhat lost in the context of this unusual moment. "I don't know you, Mr. Wren, so that feels somewhat inappropriate."

And then he smiled but smiled in a way that did indeed unveil sparks of light in his dark eyes. "Inappropriate," he repeated with a bit of a low chuckle, "as bad as all that?"

She looked away and took a sharp breath. This certainly wasn't her place. It was Colleen's. She was well out of her depth. "I meant to say I'm only here to show you Mr. Segretti's collection. That is the extent of my function here."

Again, an elusive smile and a bit of a nod. "So, I should get on with it."

"I suppose. Just into the next room are a collection of 17th-century painters from the era known as the Northern Renaissance."

"Please lead the way, Miss Brandt," he commented lightly. And she did, walking forward and not consciously considering the fact that neither she nor Mr. Segretti that she knew of had given him her last name.

The tour of the third floor stretched on as a sort of protracted aberration. Daniel Wren would pause, study a painting, examine the research booklet on the piece, then slowly and methodically move on to the next. Deborah hung back, deliberately giving him adequate space for his perusal and maintaining a distance she felt more comfortable with. Because he did, this man did make her feel profoundly uncomfortable for some inexplicable reason, even other than his unpredictable behavior. It was an odd sensation. She wasn't precisely anxious but weirdly disembodied. At times, it felt like dizziness, but at others, it felt like something else, a strange, distracted mellowness. She didn't usually feel this way on the third floor. In fact, quite the opposite. Most of the time, it elicited great irritation and discomfort in her. That was why she'd avoided it. But today, well today was different in all respects, and the only thing she could attribute it to was this man, this very unusual man, whose company she had spent the better part of an hour in.

She attempted to analyze things as she waited across the room from him. She wasn't sure if she found him attractive. Aesthetically yes, she supposed he must be so. He had thick blondish hair, not incredibly short nor long, just sort of lightly brushing the collar of his shirt. He wasn't incredibly muscular, but for some reason, though she couldn't say why, she suspected he was strong, although he was slender. He glanced up at her from the papers on an 18th-century painting of a Swedish village he was studying. It startled her. In fact, it caught her off guard as though he was responding to her thoughts. "I hope I'm not keeping you too long."

"No, no, it's fine," she smiled, that professional smile she used here at the gallery, although it felt a bit shakier and more artificial at the moment.

And then his attention returned to his reading. She tried to think about what she needed to do, but her mind was too confused and distracted. Taking out her phone, she examined it awkwardly, just to give her something else to think about.

"Miss Brandt."

She glanced up, hesitantly putting the phone back into her skirt pocket. "Yes."

He replaced the booklet he'd been holding onto the easel next to the painting. "I believe I'm finished for now. I'd like to spend a little time considering what I've seen today and email Mr. Segretti in a few days."

She smiled again, "Yes, of course, I'll take you back downstairs." Without getting an answer, she began to walk back to the doorway at the end of the long exhibition room. But then she stopped abruptly when she unexpectedly felt his hand on her arm. She hadn't sensed him moving so quickly to reach her, but the contact, the contact felt more than a bit startling — startling enough to make her stop in her tracks.

"Miss Brandt," he said quietly. "I wonder if I might ask you something."

She'd turned to him, but his hand, though not directly on her skin, was still softly gripping her forearm atop the silky blouse she wore. "Yes, what is it Mr. Wren?" She didn't smile this time. She didn't know why, except that somehow that facade had dripped away in the tenseness of the moment.

"I was wondering if I could take you out tonight for dinner."

She hesitated, a bit stunned because this she hadn't expected at all. He was asking her out. "Oh," she murmured.

And then he smiled, removing his hand. "I know it's sudden, but I find I would very much like to get to know you better."

It was confusing. She wasn't at all sure what she should or could say. It was so out of left field, and yet, "I . . . I'm closing tonight. The gallery closes at five, and then I need to get my car home. It's in a lot and—"

"Then, I could pick you up from your house around six."

Breathless, all of this felt oddly disorienting. She wasn't sure, but then again, why didn't she just say no? "Six-fifteen," she answered softly.

He nodded, "Six-fifteen, good."

She smiled, perhaps she thought, but wasn't sure. This was jarring. What was she doing? She didn't know him, but somehow certainly didn't know how to say no to him either.

<h1 style="text-align:center">The Difference</h1>

Chapter Four

The days were overcast, and it bothered her, bothered her somewhere inside her skin. At times, the city energized her, and at other times seemed to sap the very life out of her. Unfortunately, now seemed to be the latter, and while she knew that these little spells didn't usually last, at the moment, there seemed to be little light at the end of the tunnel.

"Where are you going?"

"Out with friends." It was just a little less than a year after she'd moved in with her aunt. At this early point, what Aunt Gena had told her about what she called her "special destiny" was spotty at best. So, her obscure sort of cautions fell predominantly on deaf ears. As it was in the case of most young people, she was quite convinced she knew best, and her aunt was just old-fashioned and out of touch.

She recalled, though, as she'd bent down to kiss Aunt Gena on the cheek, she'd caught Deborah's wrist with her hand, squeezing it almost painfully. "Be careful," she'd nearly rasped at her in a disconcerting way. "You're not like everyone else."

She was twenty-three at that time, a very innocent twenty-three, which vexed her a bit. Her friends, the ones she'd become close to since she'd started school in the city, had all been in and out of relationships. But Deborah had been different. Yes, there had been a few dates here and there, but nothing had come of it. She wondered if it was her, a vibe she was putting out there. That had been Margo's conclusion, the girl she was meeting tonight. "You seem so aloof, Debby, kind of cold in a way. I think you just scare the guys, make them think you're just not interested."

And then she'd wondered. Was she interested? The truth was she'd never met anyone she was particularly drawn to or rather attracted to. But tonight was an experiment. Margo's boyfriend was bringing a friend, and they were meeting at The Taproom on Magazine Street. And Deborah had decided that things would be different.

That night she drank beer, although she didn't particularly like it. Margo had ordered a pitcher with some nachos. Deborah was determined to fit in for a change. Thomas Stratford was his name, a computer science major. She remembered those details in recollection but not much else.

The Taproom, by nature, was loud and crowded, and their group sat crunched at a small round table. There were literally people everywhere, everywhere she looked, brushing her bare arms, bumping into her chair as they passed by — and noise, so much dizzying noise.

Margo had laughed frequently, talked with animation, sat next to Deborah, and nudged her with her arm from time to time. And on the other side was Thomas, Tom, bending nearer to her, asking her questions, talking, talking. And she, well, she was bolted down to her chair, feet cemented to the ground, because she had to concentrate fully, or she would run. Her skin crawled. Her head pounded. Her stomach was flipping with inexplicable nausea. And then Tom had reached over, grabbing her hand for some reason. She didn't know why, but she instinctively yanked it away because the contact with his skin actually repulsed her.

Quickly and dizzyingly, she made excuses, saying she had to leave over confused objections. She didn't know what they said, if they accepted it, or even if she was being horribly rude. She'd just stood up and left.

But Tom Stafford followed her into the parking lot, had followed her to her car.

"Hey Deborah, are you all right?" But she wasn't. She was sick and stupid, stupid for trying. Her aunt was right. She wasn't at all like everyone else. But not in a good way, not at all like her aunt made it seem.

"I just need to get home."

And then he'd tried, "Look, can I call you?" putting his hands on her arms, then leaning in to kiss her. But she pulled away sharply, sick from the contact, sick from the knowledge that all this was a failure.

What had she said? She couldn't remember. But then, in later days, she'd avoided any contact with him and Margo as well. She simply cut ties with the whole business.

She'd given him, Daniel Wren, her address and phone number. After his unexpected request, they traveled back downstairs to the main floor in the small dark elevator in virtual silence. Her mind was reeling. She supposed she should find a way to back out, back out of the dinner that he'd talked her into. But no, that wasn't exactly true. He hadn't really talked her into anything, just asked, although he definitely caught her off guard. She'd seen no indication during their brief time together that this was even a possibility. Of course, she'd been asked out before, mainly by those she attended classes with. Still, there were always indications, flirtations, that she often rebuffed, instinctively perhaps — certainly not because of her aunt's proclamations but because she wanted to keep her life simple.

But him, this stranger, she'd agreed to a date with. Then again, maybe it was just a dinner, a friendly dinner — not really a date at all.

When they'd arrived at her desk at the front of the gallery, he'd stood there, just sort of watching her calmly. "I'll need your address." He spoke quietly, not really that the volume was low, but he spoke calmly, not excitedly, nor with much tangible emotion that seemed tangled up in the speech of most people of her acquaintance, except, of course, Aunt Gena. She, too, had been calm and deliberate when she spoke.

"Oh, of course," she said, still flustered. She grabbed one of the gallery business cards and started writing her address on it with one of the pens she used at her workstation. There were always notes to be taken for any number of things: messages, appointments, but rarely, actually, never what she was using it for now. She hesitated after she wrote the address. "I'll put down my phone as well, just in case there's any change of plans." She straightened up from her slightly bent position over the desk and handed him the card.

Smoothly, he took it from her, just slightly brushing her fingertips in a way she could honestly describe as unsettling. "Thank you, Deborah," he said. "I look forward to it." And then he'd turned and left. She sank down in the burgundy velvet, wingback chair behind her desk. She didn't understand what was going on, why she felt undeniably as though the breath had been knocked out of her.

"There is a woman."

He'd laughed a bit impulsively. "Care to be more specific?"

His Uncle Silas looked at him with the slightest mark of disapproval that told him unequivocally, at least in his mind, that this was no laughing matter. As he remembered, he was twenty-two, finishing his bachelor's degree in history at the University of Missouri. Next year, as his uncle had told him, they would begin traveling to expand his education further. "This is important for you to consider, Daniel. We've discussed your unique position in this family in the past and that your companion in this will be someone who has been preselected for you."

He leaned back in the great overstuffed brown leather club chair that was in front of the fireplace of his uncle's study. They were playing a game of chess and having a brandy as was often their custom in the evenings. "All of this sounds rather antiseptic and archaic. What exactly are you saying?"

His uncle frowned. He was an unusual man. Sometimes he was extraordinarily tactful, and others as blunt as a poorly sharpened sledgehammer. "You've been told you have to be very particular about who you conduct an intimate relationship with."

"Who I sleep with?" And he'd found he could meet him for bluntness.

"Yes, that is true enough for everyone, but I might say in particular those who are anointed must, for lack of a better word, mate with their kind."

He was twenty-two, and in some ways, he had to admit, that came with a particular attitude as though one knew it all by virtue of age. Of course, as he was to learn strenuously at times, life would remold and pull one down from that assumption. "My kind?" and what exactly would be his kind.

"There is a girl out there who has been identified. We believe she could be the one for you." He sipped his brandy. Of course, he respected his uncle greatly. But he had to admit that he had been tempted to occasionally depart from his lifestyle and pursue entanglements with the opposite sex. But when he thought to do so, something would rein him in, something internally that spoke of danger.

"You know, this all smacks of an arranged relationship."

"I understand that it's different, quite different from the cultural norms of your age. But just because knowledge is old doesn't mean it's faulty. Too many people disregard the spiritual component of life to their detriment." And he knew without question when his uncle said spiritual, it had nothing to do with modern religion but something else entirely.

He sighed inwardly. He knew this older and admittedly wiser man was more than correct, but this didn't always make his dictates easy for him to live with. "This girl, does she understand all of this?"

"It's unclear. But the women of the order, whether formally initiated or not, have stronger internal protection than even the men."

"Why is that?"

"Because in straying from the path, the consequences to their spiritual health are even greater."

"Really?" he'd replied, though this wasn't actually new information for him. Over the years, he'd been extensively schooled in the connectedness between spiritual health and physical life. "When will I meet her?"

"Not for some time yet. She's young, but when you do, you must understand that the draw you will have to each other will be inescapable."

He sipped his brandy, focusing, feeling something intangibly intriguing now about the future. "And you're advising caution?"

"On the contrary, my boy, I'm advising at that time it's important you observe no caution and follow your instincts completely."

She was guarded, he'd found. Though her veneer was as transparent as the thinnest coat of lacquer that could, and if he had anything to say about it, would be easily stripped away. Physically, she seemed delicate, slender, average height for a woman, fair-skinned, with reddish-brown hair, enormous green-brown eyes, and high cheekbones. It had occurred to him that she wouldn't be totally out of place with the proper wardrobe in one of those early Northern Renaissance paintings that he'd so diligently been perusing. Though overall, she struck him as someone who might either stand out dramatically in a group or blend into the wallpaper depending on exactly which mood struck her.

And beyond all this, she did feel something about him. He could sense it in his skin as he examined the paintings on the third floor of the Sauveterre Gallery — paintings, he might add, that he had no interest whatsoever in. His interest instead was in the naturally elegant receptionist who was working hard to play a part for him, a part that he was not inclined to engage with.

He could, of course, buy a painting, in fact, any number of paintings from the gallery if he desired. He managed a rather large fund of wealth from his family line and oversaw investing and reinvesting the money to keep it well-protected as well as actively growing. That was his full-time job now, while his other pursuits took much of his energy and concentration.

Deborah Brandt had worked hard not to look at him too closely. Because when she did, he could feel it acutely, feel it on his skin, feel the energy of it as if her very delicate fingertips were brushing him, well, just about everywhere. But her thoughts were also distracting. He could feel their intensity, their confusion about precisely what it was that she was experiencing. Confusing, yes, as he deliberately blocked her full realization of who he was and who he would be to her.

There were, however, things he could tell. His uncle was right. She was, for lack of a better word, untouched, and as he had lived his life thus far ostensibly as a monk, they would mesh well in that regard.

And she was battling other things in addition, her sensitivity to her environment for one. The gallery was a difficult place for someone of her abilities, yet so untutored, to be. The energies were too strong and too difficult. While they were together, he attempted to buffer her a bit. But it was something that would have to be addressed at some point.

Yes, he was getting ahead of himself because the truth was before anything could be, anything could begin, he had to win her over.

The Date

Chapter Five

When Deborah got home, she immediately changed out of her work clothes. She had no idea where they'd be going tonight, so she chose middle of the road, a long flowing floral gypsy skirt and long-sleeve black silky blouse over it — of course, with boots, her typical attire. She pulled her reddish-brown hair up into a soft bun and put on a pair of long silver dangling earrings and a long chain with her aunt's pendant. It was a silver dove, one diving upside down. It had felt unseasonably chilly outside this evening, so she brought out a black crocheted shawl, then waited nervously in the den with a bird's eye view of the front door.

It was at this moment that she finally took a breath. And the question filtered in. What was she doing?

The clock on the wall read several minutes after six. There might still be time to beg off, something that had crossed her mind on the drive home about a hundred times. Various scenarios had crept in. She was ill, or she could sneak upstairs and simply not answer the doorbell.

Why hadn't she gotten his cell number? That would have made it so much easier to cancel. Then again, why had she even agreed? He'd caught her off-guard. She wasn't quick on her feet. Really, why was she going out with this complete stranger? Maybe it was Mr. Segretti. He seemed on such friendly terms with Mr. Wren. Perhaps that was why she'd accepted. She didn't want to jeopardize her employer's relationship with a potential client. That was an explanation, but deep down, it rang a little false, just didn't fit.

The front doorbell chimed, jarring her out of her erratic contemplations. Her heart was racing. Decide — upstairs or plunge in. She was frozen. This really wasn't that big a deal. It was only dinner, after all.

So, taking a breath, she made the decision. She opened the door. And he was standing there on her aunt's porch, looking essentially the same as he had earlier in the day.

"Hello, Deborah."

She smiled, feeling terribly awkward. The truth of the matter was she hadn't dated much at all, and it had always felt unnatural to her. "Come in," she murmured, stepping back, "I'll just get my things."

She had no idea if he'd followed behind her as she headed into the den to pick up her purse and the long black shawl from a nearby chair. But when she turned around, Daniel Wren was now standing in the middle of the room and looking around as though he were slowly examining every nuance of his surroundings.

"Whose house was this?" he said quietly.

"Who—," a bit stunned at the question. "It was my aunt's house," she answered.

"She lived here alone?"

"Yes, until I came to stay with her several years before her death."

Then he focused on her. It struck her succinctly at this moment, almost as a revelation. He was a handsome man. It was strange, as though she hadn't really seen it until just now. "You were close," maybe a statement more than a question.

"Yes," she said, "she was very good to me. I miss her a great deal."

He nodded slowly in acknowledgment. "My uncle raised me. He is also very special."

She smiled, struck awkwardly by the strange parallel in their affections and uncomfortable with his steady gaze, unsure what to say. "Where are we going?"

He looked at her warmly, and for the first time, she felt a surge of familiarity that made no sense. "I have something in mind."

There was something in the air, the night air — a shifting of energies all around them that was concerning. And Deborah Brandt was noticeably quiet. He'd parked his black Jeep Wrangler outside her home, which he'd escorted her to once they'd descended the front steps of her aunt's house.

Definitively, as soon as he stepped inside, he felt that this was her aunt's home. Genevieve Brevard's essence still dominated this place. He was sure she still watched over it even though she had shed her mortal coil. Houses, he'd found, were a strange commodity. A property could change hands many times and still be dominated by the essence of its original owner, or a new owner, maybe twentieth down the line, could take possession and completely dominate the structure as though it had been virtually untouched until their occupation. It had much to do with energy, much to do with the personal blueprints of one's life. What he knew for sure was this was not really Deborah Brandt's house. She was still a lodger in her aunt's home and would be so until she found where she truly belonged.

As they settled in the front seat of his jeep, she began to speak. He had the distinct impression she'd been working up the courage to articulate what she wanted to say. "I was surprised. I mean surprised that you asked me out to dinner. In the gallery, I, well, I didn't expect—"

He started the engine and then began to drive through the darkness. "There's an Italian restaurant near the river bend that I thought I'd take you to unless you don't like Italian."

"No, that sounds fine," she answered hesitantly.

"Good, so I'm sure you're expecting a response about the why of things."

"It would be nice." She said softly, and he decided at that moment that he liked the texture of her voice. It wasn't something he'd contemplated in the gallery. There were too many other considerations he was juggling. But now, he could relax just a bit and appreciate things.

He answered lightly, "I wish I could give you a concrete answer, Deborah, but the truth is, from the moment I laid eyes on you, I felt you were someone I needed to get to know. I have a habit of making snap decisions about some things. I hope that will suffice for now."

She shifted in the seat beside him, relaxed? That he wasn't sure of. "Yes, I mean, that's fine. After all, it's only dinner."

"So then, there's no one else?"

An awkward pause, or was it confusion? "No one?"

"Another man, boyfriend, involvement?"

He heard her take almost a startled breath. Too direct? Damn, he did have an issue in that area. "No, there's no one. I wouldn't be here with you if there was."

"Sorry, I didn't mean to embarrass you. But I'm just surprised. You're such a beautiful woman. Hard to believe there is no one in your life."

"Believe what you like, Mr. Wren. But it simply isn't the case."

Mr. Wren? That was definitely heading in the wrong direction. "Please, Daniel."

"All right," but she didn't use his name in that moment.

She felt so peculiar, so very inexplicably out of sorts. It wasn't exactly as if she felt uncomfortable with Daniel Wren, not an ordinary sort of uncomfortable. It was more as though she felt a bit altered with him. Physically, there was a weird feeling of near dizziness she was experiencing and puzzling sensations cascading across her skin, sensations that she could only describe as an awareness, but an awareness of what exactly she couldn't begin to say. And the man himself, the one who had asked her on the drive to the restaurant if she were "involved" with another man, was having this very bizarre effect on her, a sort of mellow effect — uncannily hypnotic.

By all means, she should have been offended by his inquiry — talk about bordering on intrusive. But strangely, it hadn't affected her that way. Unsettling, yes, but unpleasant? No, instead somewhat intriguing. But then again, maybe she was just overtired, and all of this would look quite different upon closer inspection.

The restaurant was Capella's. She'd passed by it often enough, a small red brick building whose entrance was flanked by voluptuous, partially clothed Grecian statues. Inside, the interior was darkened and cozy, and Daniel was immediately intercepted by a waiter, who greeted them rather quickly upon their entrance. As they exchanged pleasantries with the gray-haired, mustached gentleman, it became clear that Daniel was on a first-name basis with the staff here. Immediately after they were seated, he'd ordered, with her agreement, a bottle of red wine, brought with a basket of Parmesan bread sticks that she had to admit were pretty heavenly.

"So, I would have to conclude that you come here often."

He smiled a bit, "From time to time, I have to admit I'm a creature of habit. I find something, or someplace I like, and tend to stick with it."

She sipped the wine, not too dry but just poised on the edge of bitterness. "But I've never seen you at the gallery before."

"No, but I am quite earnest in acquiring a painting."

"Any painting?"

"One that I feel would be a good investment."

"So, you're not in it for the aesthetic pleasure?"

He eyed her speculatively, oddly, as if he was enjoying her questioning. "Historical value, yes, aesthetic? Well, that's not the primary consideration."

"I see," absorbing the information in an attempt to get a more rounded picture of her dinner companion.

"Though I have to admit I do appreciate beauty in other arenas."

She looked at him with a bit of surprise. Clearly, that was directed at her. And it felt awkward, though he delivered it smoothly enough. She wasn't used to compliments or flirting or whatever this might be. Though actually, it didn't feel like that. It just felt like something he was thinking. From her brief exposure to him, she was getting the impression he was a bit on the uncensored side.

She sipped her wine, considering exactly how to respond. "So, on the drive over, you asked me if I had a boyfriend or an involvement. What about you? Can I make the same inquiry?" She said this rather matter-of-factly, wanting to shift the focus of the conversation.

But his dark eyes settled on her, and again she felt that strange stirring of recognition. Had they met before, and she'd just forgotten? "The answer is no, Deborah. There is no one, nothing of that sort, in my life now. And I might add as you did that I wouldn't be here with you if there were."

"But we're only having dinner," she laughed a bit, trying to diffuse the moment's intensity.

"Yes, of course, that's true." Fortunately, she didn't have to consider a response as the waiter arrived interrupting. And in retrospect, she thought that was for the best.

"I can hear it sometimes. It sounds like howling in my ears."

"Like wolves?"

"No, like the wind swirling in a storm with a high-pitched whistling."

"It's the low ones approaching."

"The low ones?"

"Yes, sometimes they band together so tightly they can manifest in our reality, permeate the barriers. It's clear you have a sense for their approach."

"What do they want?"

"Life force, to destroy and drain the flesh-shrouded ones."

"Flesh-shrouded?"

"Us, my boy."

It was unnerving. Sometime during their dinner, it had begun, softly at first, then increasing, increasing now to the point where it was like a sharp pain in his ears. "Daniel, don't ignore the warnings."

He remembered his uncle always coaching him to develop his gifts and fine-tune his sensitivities. What was becoming abundantly clear to him was that this evening would not quite go the way he'd planned.

He put down his utensils and lightly touched Deborah's arm. She looked up in surprise from the plate of crawfish fettuccine that she was only half done with. Her large hazel eyes were wide, and she asked softly. "What is it?"

"I'm so sorry about this, but we must leave right now."

"Oh," she seemed shaken as she lowered her utensils, "are you all right?"

"I'll explain once we get in the car. But for now, you'll just have to trust me." He pulled out a hundred-dollar bill, and a fifty that he was more than certain was in great excess of their charges, dropped it on the table, and stood up. She followed his lead, standing and pulling on her shawl that she'd laid across the chair beside her. Taking her hand, then nodding to the waiter, he quickly ushered her out the front door.

There was a shift as he felt the cool night air hit him and heard a great rustle of bird wings that he did not see. *"They sense you together and want to stop you."*

He put his arm around Deborah, trying to pull her quickly along, though she seemed more than accommodating in keeping up with his step. As they walked down the darkened street to the car, shadows seemed to shift around them, almost discernible but not quite. Unlocking the doors, he quickly pulled her door open, and she jumped in, pulling it closed. She waited for him to follow, which he did quickly, starting the engine the moment that the doors were locked.

"Where are we going?" she asked as he began to drive, not what's wrong, or why are we leaving.

"I can't take you home yet."

He thought he saw her nod but couldn't be sure because her face was shrouded in darkness.

Chapter Six

She wondered at times if she believed her aunt, the stories about the Gauthier bloodline: the stories about her being different, the mark on her neck, the need to find someone, a man who was "suited" to her, and the idea that there was a greater purpose in her life than just the ones that everyone sought — a home, a career, a family, someone to love.

It was easy at times to just ignore these fanciful ideas that her aunt had planted in her mind, but then things would happen. There were the dreams during which people would be talking to her, almost counseling her in some way, and she'd awake with only shadows of memory. And also, there were feelings, "sensitivities," as her Aunt Gena had described. And there was also her ingrained repulsion toward any intimacy with a man or even a woman. And then, there was tonight.

She'd looked up into Daniel Wren's eyes and felt a tangible fear travel down her spine. And it wasn't his fear, but something else, something very close to them. As they traveled through the darkness, her breathing felt labored as though some great pressure was pressing on her chest, and at the same time, on her forehead, on the middle, what her aunt had called the third eye.

"Why? Why can't you take me back to my house?" she asked. Even her voice sounded breathless in her ears.

"Because they will track you there, and it must remain hidden."

She leaned back in the seat, her head spinning. What had he said? "Who are they?"

"You need to relax right now Deborah. Close your eyes and try to rest." It was so strange. His voice sounded so strong in her ears that as soon as he'd said it, she felt a grogginess overtake her. She wanted to say, "Wait a minute? What are you talking about?" But it was impossible because she was already falling into a light sleep.

Here, it was daytime as she walked through the small, deserted playground. It was a place she recognized, somewhere off Banks St. But it was different, so quiet now. Usually, it was active — busy with traffic on the adjacent streets or young children running across the well-worn pathways around the swing sets, see-saws, and picnic tables. But now, as she silently moved through its interior, she noted how worn and ill-kept it all seemed.

Except, of course, for the birds, the crows sitting on the iron bars, six, seven, perhaps more restlessly hopping from convenient fixture to fixture. And as she watched them, her long black nightgown dragged across the damp grass.

"What is this?" she wondered aloud.

"They are harbingers." She heard his voice first, then opened her eyes. It was Daniel who'd spoken. And as she glanced around, she realized that the car had stopped. In fact, they were inside some sort of parking garage. She'd slept through this, getting here.

"What did you say?" she asked in confusion.

"Come on. We need to get inside for a bit," he said as he turned off the car and undid his seatbelt. He hadn't answered her, but then again, maybe that had just been part of a dream.

"I need to get home," she murmured, her voice and every inch of her feeling out of sync.

"Don't worry. I'll get you back there as soon as it's possible."

This one was near the lakefront, a condo that he used occasionally. He'd found it more than necessary living in this city to have several residences. In a tangible way, it made it more confusing as to where he was living and when.

Deborah Brandt had not shut down on him yet, and for that, he was grateful. And she hadn't asked too many questions, and for that, he was relieved. He'd expected their first official contact to be challenging but hadn't realized it would be a full-out siege.

She walked beside him quietly, still seeming disoriented from the heavy sleep she'd awoken from. If he were any other man acting as he had tonight, he would expect her to run as far away as possible. But she hadn't, and he knew that was because somewhere deep down already, she could feel the connection between them. They entered the elevator heading up to the seventh floor.

"You live here?" she asked somewhat calmly.

"Tonight, it would seem so," he answered.

She looked at him with little reaction. His curious wit, as his uncle had often told him, was an acquired dish.

And then she glanced away, trying to collect her thoughts, he assumed. He knew that she was feeling much, in truth, more than he'd expected. The elevator smoothly eased to a stop, and the door silently whooshed open. She didn't move, just remained still. She seemed so dazed, caught up in an altered state since she'd slept. Well, even though it was making her more compliant, it unnerved him. He grabbed her arm firmly with his hand. "Come on," he murmured, and again she began to move beside him.

"So, you never married?"

Aunt Gena looked up at her with her sharp, smoky blue eyes, eyes, not seeming surprised at the question. Although

Deborah honestly didn't ever remember her being surprised at much of anything, she'd ever asked. "In a conventional sense, no not really."

Deborah mulled that over. What exactly did she mean in a conventional sense? "So, you were never really involved in a serious relationship?"

She smiled and put down her knitting. It was a curious phenomenon that once her aunt's illness had ensued, she'd taken up knitting at almost a furious pace. The two scarves and throw that Deborah now possessed attested to the fact. "Now, I never said that. There was a serious involvement I had, brief though it was."

Deborah sank down in the seat beside her aunt's rocking chair. "Really? How serious?"

Then those cool blue eyes had shot her a particularly sharp glance. "Now that my darling would be none of your business."

"But I thought you said something about it being very important who we became intimately involved with, something about the bloodline."

And then her aunt had picked up her knitting needles again as if to signal that this conversation had ended. "Yes, indeed it is."

It was bright, his house or, rather, his condo. But she could still see the birds, black crows, or ravens settling on the tops of the swing sets, the monkey bars of the children's gymnasium.

He was holding her arm, ushering her into a large room, the walls seeming just a tinge off-white, and there was a curving brown couch facing a cold fireplace where he led her to sit. She could still hear them and see them as she turned. There was the rustle of the black wings all around her, and then she glanced up. They were here, inside, nestled in the empty fireplace, walking along the off-white built-in shelves along the walls, just a few books and the crows walking, hopping about. He pinched her arms. He was crouching in front of her pinching both her arms and shaking her. "Focus Deborah, don't allow them in. Focus on where you are."

Harder now, it was painful, and he was shaking her. She could hear them shrieking, ugly shrieking, in her ears. He yanked her to her feet, still shaking her, pinching her painfully. "Come on, get hold," he rasped.

And then she yanked away from his grasp, abruptly snapping at him. "Stop it! That hurts."

He stepped back from her, looking a bit more satisfied. "Okay, that's better."

She looked around as if for seeing for the first time, completely jolted. "What is this place?" They were in a long room, a den she surmised, with chairs, dark brown, the couch she'd just been jolted up from, the built-in shelves around the off-white fireplace, a large painting on one wall of the New Orleans lighthouse, and not much else.

And Daniel Wren was standing in front of her, very close, looking a bit disheveled after their last exchange. "This is my home."

Then she looked at him with confusion, "No, no, this isn't."

He stared at her and then smiled almost with a look of admiration. "Well, you have me there. Let me make some coffee. Then we'll talk a bit."

What do you see?"

"Birds."

"Kind?"

"Birds in flight, perched, and—"

"And?"

"Dead, some on the ground."

"Freshly dead?"

He shifted a bit. His legs were starting to cramp in his seated position on the throw rug at the foot of his bed. "Is that important?"

"Everything is important. Every detail may have symbolic consequence."

He exhaled, attempting to crystallize his vision somewhat. "Yes, freshly dead, I would say, no rotting corpses."

"This is not a time for levity Daniel." This was his mother's voice in his mind, not actually with him. But they did meditate together, even though she was far away at her spiritual commune or sanctuary, as Uncle Silas had called it. They had fixed a time every Thursday at seven in the evening. He would meditate, and she would join in, schooling him on the significance of his visions or whatever the consideration of the day might be. He'd found her to be quite exacting about their meetings too. He'd canceled a few times and was met with a bit of disdain from his absentee parent, so he'd tried henceforth to make these appointments. This one occurred only a week ago.

"I wouldn't call it levity, perhaps a sprinkling of sarcasm."

"The birds you see, what color are they?"

"They are black, always black crows or ravens perhaps, though ravens only travel in pairs."

"These aren't normal circumstances. The birds will not be following their ordinary patterns. They are being influenced." There was a hesitation. She was considering. He could feel it. These mediations enabled him to be near his mother's thoughts and feelings, though she seemed to work hard to keep these in check. "All black birds?"

Again, he focused intently on his vision. It would fluctuate, ripple with uncertainty in moments, then settle down again. "Seems so."

"There will be a white bird. Watch for it. It will signal the beginning."

Deborah Brandt's head was beginning to clear. She'd been on a date with Daniel Wren, and now she was in his condominium for some inexplicable reason, although it seemed she had come here of her own free will. She drifted from the genuinely sparsely decorated den toward the open kitchen where he had disappeared some minutes before.

Besides being somewhat confused about what was happening, her head ached a bit, and there was a perceptible dizziness clinging to her. Pausing near the entranceway of the kitchen for a moment, she watched. He'd divested himself of his sports jacket, and his back was to her. Evidently, he was pouring out that coffee he'd mentioned.

"Go ahead," he said. Then he turned around, facing her. "You wanted to say something."

"I'm feeling a bit confused."

He frowned ever so slightly, "I didn't, you know."

"Didn't what?" she questioned.

"Slip anything into your wine, drug you. That's what you're wondering."

"No, I—" then she stopped. It had crossed her mind. Things like that were not unheard of.

"How do you like your coffee?" he asked, clearly content to brush aside the awkwardness from the moment before.

"Oh," she sighed uncomfortably, "a little milk, teaspoon of sugar." He turned back to the counter to complete the task.

"You know, I'd rather you be candid, honest. I'm not offended," he said, turning round again and handing the steaming mug to her.

"How can you not be offended by being accused of drugging someone?"

"Was I accused?"

"No, I just feel confused, and that's not normal for me."

"Well, just to be clear, honesty doesn't bother me."

She took a sip out of the beige mug that oddly felt keenly as though it might be brand new and completely unused. The coffee was strong, a bit on the bitter side laced with chicory, just as she liked it. And it did help to sharpen her senses that had felt unusually dulled not so many moments before. "This helps, but I don't understand."

He took a sip of his coffee and looked at her thoughtfully while leaning back against the gray granite top counter. "Don't understand what exactly, Deborah?"

"I don't understand why we're here, why we left the restaurant so abruptly and are now here."

A fleeting smile passed across his lips and then seemed to vanish at least as quickly. "I suppose it's too much to believe I just wanted to be alone with you."

She frowned a bit. She couldn't help it. "Um, well, that's interesting, but I don't really buy it. It felt as though we were somehow fleeing something."

He put his mug down on the counter. "Fleeing, interesting word," he said as he moved closer to her. "So, you tell me, Deborah. What do you think we might have been fleeing?"

His eyes seemed strange to her, dark, obsidian-like, piercing, making her think again about the dreams—

"Dreams?" he murmured. "While you slept in the car, what were you dreaming about?"

"I—" it wasn't registering, not completely that she hadn't said the word dreams aloud, but he had. Daniel Wren had voiced it aloud. "It was the birds, black birds, crows, or something. Was that what you were fleeing?" she asked, though to hear it, the question was purely nonsensical.

"No, not exactly, though they are markers for what is coming."

"What is—" then she stopped. She felt strange, as though everything around her was so insubstantial. "Who are you?" she whispered as the cold realization of all the dangling threads and unanswered questions hit her acutely.

He seemed to hesitate as though carefully considering his answer. "Deborah, your aunt told you I would be coming to help you, partner with you in some respects, and guide you through difficult times."

And then he slowly reached up to where his collar was on the right side of his neck and pulled it down. Her eyes widened at what she was seeing. It was the mark, the same birthmark on his neck except situated opposite of hers, as though a mirror image. "The paladin," she whispered, not really meaning to, but it slipped out.

"Paladin, archaic term but yes, in some respects, I suppose that is what we are," he said with a curious smile that made her feel as though her reality had just been torn away like tissue paper.

"This is impossible," she said shakily, "and my aunt was ill."

He stared at her intently for a moment as though considering, then pulled his collar back up around his neck. "Would you like to sit, Deborah?" he said calmly, as though not truly acknowledging what she had said.

"I'd like to go home."

She was frightened, truly frightened, and why shouldn't she be, he wondered. Life as she knew it, or rather attempted to know it, was about to shift dramatically. He walked past her back into the quiet den and sat on the long mocha-colored couch. Either she would follow him, or she wouldn't. He glanced around. That was what he did not like about this place. It was too quiet, too void of a cacophony of energies. But that also was what made it useful, he supposed.

She drifted into the room, coffee still in hand, and sat in the brown club chair near the sofa, not beside him. He frightened her. Well, that was just as well. In many respects, she frightened him, though not in ways he was quite ready to define.

"She wasn't always ill."

"No," she said softly. "But this—" then she stopped, unable to frame the words.

He put his coffee on the long glass table in front of the sofa. He'd lost his taste for it. "So, tell me a bit about your life Deborah."

"My life?" she said with confusion. He was sensing things. She was afraid but not exactly afraid of him per se. She was very afraid of what she was feeling.

"Yes." He didn't elaborate. He didn't want to guide her in any way.

"I—I go to school, and I work. Sometimes I see friends."

"Do you date?"

She shifted in the chair. It made her uncomfortable, the question. "Sometimes," she murmured. "What do you want from me?"

"Me? Nothing really," well, that wasn't true. He actually needed quite a bit from her, but he didn't want to scare her. "Your aunt, what did she say about the mark on you?"

"She said that I would have to live my life differently, that I might be called into service. Is this what you're doing here? Calling me into some kind of service?"

It was clear. He was canvassing the images that were accompanying her words. She hadn't told her much, just the bare bones, and perhaps just enough to help keep her out of trouble. "That's one way of looking at it, I suppose. The truth is things are happening now in this city that I need your help with."

"How, how do you think I could help?"

He looked at her. She was too far away. He needed to be closer but not scare her. He stood and walked toward her, standing in front of the chair. Her eyes were wide, her heart beating loudly in tandem with her distress. He could see now that it would have been better if he'd gone about this differently, simply pursued a relationship with her first and eased into this. Perhaps, he thought to himself. Perhaps, he could still build in that area. He reached in, taking the cup of coffee from her hands and putting it on the end table beside her.

He listened acutely, listened with his senses. Around them, he could feel a quiet now. The immediate danger had passed. Next time, he could anticipate what had occurred, perhaps keep them more camouflaged.

Boldly, he took her hands, gently pulling her to her feet. "I," but then she stopped because he'd lightly put his finger over her lips.

"It's all right, Deborah," he murmured. "We'll start this again." And then he softly pulled her into his arms and began to kiss her. Her body stiffened in shock, but he soothed her with his hands on her back and shoulders, and she began to relax. He deepened the kiss, desperately wanting to take more. But he didn't. He needed to backtrack a bit.

A Different Approach

Chapter Seven

"So, where were you last night? I left messages. I wanted to see if you wanted to catch a movie."

"Oh, sorry, I didn't really check my phone."

Jessica looked at her oddly. They'd met for coffee just before her 8:00 a.m. European History class that morning. "And?" she added a bit emphatically.

"And?" she repeated. They were sitting outside at a table at the French Express coffee shop just across from the library, where begrudgingly, she acknowledged that she should be researching the paper due at the end of the week.

Jessica stirred her frothy cafe mocha and looked at her with a bit of disdain. "And where were you? And don't tell me you were taking a bath. I called several times."

A montage of images rushed before her eyes, images that Deborah wasn't at all sure she cared to share. Upon closer inspection this morning, a less than tangible, unreal quality still lingered over last night's events. "I actually went out to dinner with someone," she said softly, curiously even reluctant to share just that much.

Jessica leaned in a bit. Her interest now somewhat peaked. "Was it Ross? He told me he was going to call you."

"No, no," she swirled her heavy paper coffee cup. "No, it was someone I met at the gallery, a friend of Mr. Segretti's."

Jessica's eyebrows darted in a bit. "Mr. Segretti? He's that old guy. How old exactly was this man?"

She smiled, "Not that old, I mean, maybe around thirty, I guess."

"Hmm," she said with a dash of skepticism, "good looking?"

She nodded, feeling somewhat regretful she'd opened this door. Honestly, she would have preferred to keep it to herself just now. "Look, it was only dinner. He asked me out to dinner, and I went. That's all." More images flashed before her eyes. Parking in front of her house — he, Daniel, escorting her to the door, then coming in, he said, for safety reasons, just to be certain everything was all right. Then, before he left, telling her softly that he wanted to see her again. Her heart fluttered a bit at the recollection. He'd pulled her into his arms and kissed her, kissed her warmly, passionately, and she'd clung to him, or was it melted against him? It wasn't like anything she'd experienced before. The truth was she didn't usually like being touched, but this was entirely different, remarkably confusing in some ways.

She refocused on the friend before her, looking at her with curiosity. "Are you going to see him again?"

"I — I really don't know."

Daniel waited. He wondered if the memories he'd altered had stuck at all. He'd taken a chance, a rather big chance, deciding to fade out the disturbing events of their date last night and add a few benign details to fill in time. Instead of being a rushed debacle, their dinner together was extended, comforting, filled with engaging conversation. Then later, the events at his condo were adapted, instead changed to time at a local coffee shop down St. Charles Avenue. All of it was quite ordinary, no conversation about their mission together, birthmarks on their respective necks, or much of anything.

Altering memories was not as rare and extraordinary as one might think. People tended to alter their own memories often for all sorts of reasons, sometimes trauma, sometimes just replacing something disturbing or upsetting with something more palatable to their sensitivities. And sometimes, just for the sake of ego, desiring a more beneficial recollection than was originally afforded them.

But his altering of Deborah's memories, he categorized as strictly utilitarian. The two of them needed to have a more solid foundation before the true intricacies of their new relationship could be opened up. But there was one thing that was very real. Last night, he'd walked into her house, an important invitation, which gave him more access than he'd ever had before, and he'd also kissed her — again. It was not like the other kiss, the one in his condominium which was more calculated. The kiss at her house was aimed at establishing a physical connection, building energy bonds between them, touching, crossing personal boundaries, and beginning to open gateways.

And in kissing her, he had to force himself to stop because the draw was so intense, nearly overwhelming. He knew she'd felt it just as strongly, but it frightened her — and frightened him as well.

Last night, she'd dreamed of her aunt. She was sure of it. They were talking, talking quite a bit, but upon waking, she couldn't remember exactly what was said. It was important. At least it felt that way, but the details had slipped away in the glare of a new morning.

Deborah allowed the flood of the day's events to fully eclipse the night before. In fact, around one o'clock in the afternoon, when he called, she'd already had a full day largely devoid of recollections from the previous evening.

"Deborah."

She'd just gotten home and was drinking a glass of iced tea. It was a habit carried over from her time living with Aunt Gena. There was always iced tea chilling in the refrigerator in one specific glass pitcher. There were so many things in the nine months that her aunt had been gone that she'd kept the same in the house. It was still as though she didn't really own the place at all, instead was a sort of a caretaker for the way her aunt wanted things done.

"Yes," she'd answered the phone with a slight bit of uneasiness. It was surprising, perhaps a little jarring, hearing from him. For some reason, she hadn't anticipated talking to him again so quickly. She'd really thought there would be time, time for her to consider, turn things over in her mind.

"I hope I haven't caught you at a bad moment."

Looking around Aunt Gena's den, it felt homey, welcoming, and secluded, honestly still acting as the refuge it had always been for her. "No, I actually just got in and was relaxing a bit."

"Are you working today?"

"Um, no, not today." Her heart was picking up its beat. It was clear what was next. He wanted to see her tonight, but she hadn't thought about things, thought about what she truly wanted.

Instinctively glancing to the corner of the room, she remembered vividly how he'd just pulled her into his arms and started kissing her as though it was natural. She hadn't expected it, but everything about this man felt unexpected.

Of course, Deborah had been kissed before but not like this. Truthfully, she'd always held back in terms of intimacy, like the debacle with Margo's friend. Impulsively, she thought about her aunt in the dream, about her aunt talking to her about something important, but she couldn't quite reach it.

"I'd like to see you tonight. Would you have dinner with me?"

She hesitated, not surprised at all because this was what she'd anticipated, but still feeling jolted, nonetheless. What did she want? It was true she was very drawn to him and enjoyed his company, even his somewhat unpredictable manner. He felt refreshing to her, often unsure what he might say or do next.

"You're quiet," he said softly. "Just dinner, just want to get to know you better."

"All right," she answered, again not fully analyzing what she really wanted.

"Good, I'll come get you at six."

He stared at his cell phone, lightly putting it on the rustic end table beside his chair. He felt deeply unsatisfied. The problem was that this tactic he had decided on might not work, perhaps not at all. Deborah was undeniably powerful in her own right. He closed his eyes, trying to clear his mind and focus, focus on what exactly was nagging at him.

Breathing deeply, he allowed himself to sink down, down into another level of reality, one that Uncle Silas called the symbolic place. It was a quiet place for him that he often used as a refuge to work out his problems. In it, he could see the sky overhead, a curious gray cloudy hue, overcast and oppressive in some regard.

It was the plane of reality closest to the surface level of the mind. The terrain for him was hilly but sloping hills, a forest, not a crowded, clustered forest but enough room to walk where overhead the high branches of the trees bent over, shrouding much of the gray sky. He concentrated on calmness, but still, the gloomy environment would not give way.

"Your heart isn't in it."

He continued to move somberly, quite fully aware that his mother was now walking beside him. She was a tall, elegant blond woman with her hair loosely pulled back in a bun. She wore a long off-white robe tied with a sky-blue sash. The colors were symbolic, linked with the energies of her aura. Beside her and keeping up with their gait was a small sheltie. He smiled at her presence, and the environment around them seemed to lighten a tad. Her name was Jolie. Uncle Silas had given her to him when she was only a pup, and they had been fast friends for so many years until she crossed over. But she did make an appearance from time to time in his meditations, in flashes, certainly in his feelings, always bringing happy remembrances with her.

Down at the end of the small winding forest path, he could see a small, quaint cottage with a chimney expelling wisps of smoke, welcoming, but he did not desire to rest just now, but rather to consider things.

"I don't know why you'd say that," he responded to her bleak pronouncement.

"You know, my son, it wouldn't kill you to be somewhat pleased that you've finally met her, the woman who undoubtedly will be pivotal in your life. But then again, you've begun the relationship being manipulative, which puts a damper on things."

He sighed. He didn't need this right now. "There are bigger things in play now. You, most of all, should understand that."

"Me, most of all? Sounds like a bit of resentment still hanging in the air Daniel."

"No, not at all. It's just a time to be pragmatic."

"Well, don't forget to feel, my boy, even while you're being pragmatic."

Reverse, Repeat

Chapter Eight

"Where are we going?" she asked, unsure why she hadn't asked before. Daniel had arrived at her door just a minute or two after six, punctual. Was that bad or good? She had no idea. Her preparations for this "date" felt oddly disoriented, as though she were operating in some sort of fog. She was tired, oddly tired, and she really had things to do for school. Perhaps, she could cut the evening short and remember not to accept another invitation. It had been her practice lately to avoid traditional dating of any sort. And she hadn't considered last night's outing an actual date, just a sort of social excursion. That was, of course, until it wasn't.

Intense and vivid memories flooded back, the kiss. He'd insisted on seeing her safely into the house. And on the one hand, the idea of this man, who she had ostensibly just met, being so protective was charming, but, on the other hand, her prudent nature made her a little apprehensive.

But he acted the perfect gentleman, until he didn't, until completely unexpectedly she was pulled into a warm embrace, kissed, and not kissed chastely.

And it wasn't as though she disliked it because she didn't. She felt— and words sort of fell away at the charging emotions and fluid sensations rushing through her skin, her blood. Erotic, yes, that would be a description.

And now, she wondered if she might need to break all of this off.

"You might have to live your life differently," her aunt's words.

Her aunt's warnings, her predictions about her life, they'd come back today or rather were dragged back with a bit of a struggle. Strangely, certain things had felt cloudy in her mind after last night, but this she fought for, forced back into consciousness with an extreme bit of focus.

"You are part of an old bloodline, my dear, and you can't just be with anyone. It would be profoundly destructive for you to do so." And then there was more, though still cloudy. There was a particular person, a partner out there for her with which she might be called upon to join forces, who would teach her to use her gifts.

Of course, if she was being honest, for the balance of the time that she'd spent with Aunt Gena, she'd viewed most of these ramblings as sheer nonsense. While being a lovely person, her aunt was ill for a large chunk of the time she was with her. So, all this destiny business was probably the product of some kind of delusion.

That was a reasonable explanation if she chose to travel in that direction. And Deborah's personal choices about involvements and relationships had been just that, her personal choices — nothing to do with this *you have to live your life differently* business.

But there was that mark on her neck, the stinging, burning, tingling mark that felt completely dormant.

All of this seemed so cumbersome right now. It had been easy before. And she hadn't been forced to sift through this strangeness. No one, no man, had truly drawn her, so avoiding connection wasn't a particular problem. But Daniel Wren was undeniably different. Just being around him felt electric and at the same time, oddly dangerous, but a danger that didn't repel but instead drew her.

In her mind, the pendulum continued to swing back and forth. In a very rational sense, complicated was not something she needed. So, she would make tonight's dinner the last. That was indeed what she should do, not considering if it was truly what she wanted.

"There's a restaurant on the lakefront."

"Olivier's," she murmured.

He smiled, "Yes, not quite as intimate as Capella's, but the view is something." They were driving through the city. Dusk had already fallen, and she wondered distantly why she felt so distracted. "Unless you'd rather go somewhere else."

She shook her head slowly. "No, that's fine."

He reached over and squeezed her hand as though in some sort of reassurance, but the contact shot that awareness through her skin, that sleepy, hypnotic awareness that she remembered so clearly from the night before. "Are you all right, Deborah?" he asked softly.

"I think so," she said, not convinced, not really convinced at all.

She was fighting it, last night's restructuring on his part. What had his mother said — something about not forgetting to feel? He could push with her, push to keep the illusion in place, but he didn't really want someone he was purely controlling at his side. She had to make up her mind about things if it turned out they had that kind of time.

They were sitting next to the large plate glass window of the restaurant. Just outside was a substantial deck and beyond the lake. Even in the darkness, he could see and feel the water's turbulence, its swirling energy. But thus far, it was nothing like last night.

"It's really beautiful here," she said. He glanced up. Her eyes were fixed on the outside, staring out at the lake as well.

"You like the water."

She looked up, eyes wide and surprised, he thought. "Yes," she smiled. "I've always toyed with the idea of getting a house right on the water one day or maybe even a houseboat."

"But that would be a complete lifestyle change."

"That wouldn't bother me. Sometimes I think it's important to be completely yanked out of your comfort zone."

He looked at her oddly, picking up the glass of Chablis in front of him. He'd ordered a bottle of wine when they arrived. "I agree," he said, bringing the cold beverage to his lips. "What else?" he said softly.

"What else?" she repeated, looking a little confused.

"Tell me what else you'd like to do that you haven't."

She smiled gently, making him think she was surprised at his request, "Maybe travel, see Europe. Have you been?"

He nodded, "Yes, a few times," thinking of the ancient power points he'd visited on the continent.

"My aunt, My Aunt Gena, told me about time she'd spent in England and France, made me envious to see it."

"You should. I'm sure you'd draw a lot out of it, though there is a lot in this city as well."

She leaned back in the chair a bit. "Do you think so, New Orleans?"

"Yes, I do. It's an old place, and people have always gravitated here for a reason, good and bad."

"Yes, I've only been here four years, but I can see that, though I confess lately I wonder if the bad has become a bit more dominant."

He took a silent breath. She was aware. It was strange. He knew she was sensitive by virtue of who she was, but it wasn't entirely dormant as he'd assumed. "Why do you say that?"

She shrugged, eyes seeming a little distant as though searching for validation for something he knew darn well she just felt, felt in her skin. "I don't know. The news, I suppose, seems to be some crime or violent episode more frequently as of late. And—"

"And?" he asked, wanting to know more, more about how her mind and emotions worked.

"And places, places in the city I used to get a charge out of. They feel different, not the same at all."

He could feel a silent expel of breath from somewhere around his lungs. "As though they're being appropriated," he elaborated.

She looked at him curiously, clearly caught by what he'd said. "I—" she hesitated, wanting to say more, he was sure. "I don't know," she murmured.

And then, the waitress arrived to take their orders. But he was intrigued, stirred. He wanted to explore more of this, much more of what was going on inside of Deborah Brandt.

Pattern

Chapter Nine

The dinner was lovely and surprising. She talked quite a bit, more than she usually did. As it was, Deborah had always considered herself somewhat reserved. And it seemed as though Daniel Wren was interested, extremely interested in what she had to say on just about everything. And he'd commented quite a bit, giving his thoughts and opinions on subjects, but she noticed he said little about his personal life.

From what she did glean, he was a businessman of some sort, managed his family's holdings, or that was what she gathered, but specifics she couldn't quite pull from him. Though quite honestly, she hadn't tried that hard.

After dinner, they went to the Café Du Monde coffee shop in City Park, and then he took her home. He was so attentive to her, being mindful that she had early morning classes and did not want to interfere with her obligations.

He was polite, but he had a curious edge, what her aunt might call a brittleness, not smooth but jagged, unpredictable.

A brittleness that, at present, didn't seem to bother her. For some reason, she'd always been suspicious of someone who was too polished, whose veneer seemed flawless. It made it difficult to see or feel who they really were.

And at the end of the evening again, he escorted her to the door, making her feel slightly off-balance when he asked to come inside. When she hesitated, he'd smiled and said it was only to ensure everything was safe and secure. With that, she'd allowed it. After all, it seemed to be rude to refuse.

And just as she remembered the night before, Daniel somewhat methodically paced the den, glancing at the windows and intently looking toward the staircase upstairs and the doorway leading to the kitchen but making no move to go anywhere else. He did appear extremely focused, focused on something that she didn't understand.

Once he finished his ritual, he looked at her again. "Make sure to lock up after I leave," he said a little sternly, almost as though he were giving her an order rather than a suggestion.

She frowned a bit, feeling distinctly as though something was not quite right here. "Of course, I always do," she murmured.

He nodded, his attention now entirely on her. "I suppose I seem like a strange fellow to you."

"Yes, maybe a bit, but I've always believed that the concept of being normal is kind of a myth anyway."

Then he'd moved closer to her. "You're right about that. There is no normal, just perception and expectations, I suppose. But I must say I'm enjoying spending time with you, Deborah." Her face felt a bit flushed at that, the directness of his manner. Then his hands were on her arms, pulling her a bit closer. It flashed across her mind. She remembered her decision earlier to put a stop to things, but somewhere during the night, all of that had sort of swirled away.

"Daniel," she said softly, struggling somewhat to articulate something.

"Yes," he whispered in her hair because he had pulled her quite close, and it felt so right, again like melting, relaxing somewhere deep inside.

"I don't know —" then she stopped because he was kissing her. He was kissing her gently at first, then continuing until she was kissing him back.

It felt so natural to be in his arms, his skin touching hers. And it would be natural and expected if there was more if he stayed with her, but he didn't. He pulled back, away from her, and undeniably a part of her was disappointed, though in her mind she knew that it was the right and correct thing.

"Goodnight," he said, kissing her briefly and chastely on the cheek. Then he'd rather abruptly opened the door and left.

She stood momentarily in the middle of the den, wondering exactly what was happening. It just felt strange, as though she was missing something. With a sigh as insisted, she bolted the door behind him, her hands trembling slightly, still feeling that palpable energy left from his embrace.

Daniel Wren hesitated on the stone porch of Deborah Brandt's house feeling visibly shaken. The draw he had to her was almost overwhelming. He'd had no idea the fortitude he would have to exercise to play her suitor. But then again, he wasn't playing at it. He was her suitor, though undeniably, he wanted much more.

An awareness passed over his skin, and he glanced across the porch, across the side yard, directly over to the house next door. It was a two-story wooden house painted the palest of cream colors. But just looking at it sent a frisson of irritation across his skin.

He frowned, potential problems so close. That was unfortunate. He would have to keep his eye on it.

"So, tell me about this guy you're dating."

She grimaced a bit. She'd woken up this morning with a bad headache and a curious lingering feeling of fatigue, which was manifesting into irritation at this particular moment. "I'd rather not, and we're not dating. I mean, it's been just a couple of dinners, nothing much."

She sipped her large, well-chilled iced tea in a tall paper cup. She'd left out the sugar and just put lemon in it. She was trying to cultivate a liking for it, but all she could taste in her mouth was bitter.

"Is he a good kisser?" She glared a bit at Jessica, who was prying for some inexplicable reason, which Deborah suspected could possibly be just sheer boredom.

"I'm not discussing this with you," she mumbled a bit coldly.

"So, he did kiss you. Did he do more?"

"Are you even listening to me?"

"You know, you never talk about this stuff with me. You always keep me at a distance."

She laughed smiling a bit. "Of course, I don't."

But, of course, she did, at least upon reflection she recognized it. She didn't share quite a bit with Jessica, her so-called closest friend. She'd listened a lot to Aunt Gena but rarely shared with her.

The truth was no one knew her, and it made her a bit uncomfortable to consider this as Daniel was getting closer.

"What are you thinking about?"

They were having dinner at a small Chinese restaurant near the lakefront. "Nothing much, really. It's strange how few Chinese restaurants you see these days."

He focused on her with a bit of humor in his eyes. "And that's what you were thinking? Moments ago, you were deep in thought."

She shook her head, "Not really, I," then stopped. He was reading her. She'd begun to notice in their limited acquaintance that he'd gotten into the habit of being in tune with her mood. "I—I was actually thinking about my aunt."

He picked up his glass of wine. It was white wine they were sharing tonight, a Pinot Grigio. "Your Aunt Gena, I imagine you miss her."

"I do. I suppose it sounds odd, but I feel her around the house a lot. I actually turn a corner or come down the stairs, and I thoroughly expect to see her, then I remember."

He looked at her intently, considering what she'd said, then commented, "That's not unexpected. I'm sure your aunt's spirit spends a lot of time with you and in the house."

Looking at him blankly, she tried to absorb what she'd heard. "Spirit? Do you mean ghost?"

"No, not a ghost," he said a bit too casually, considering the subject. "A ghost is someone who has not moved onto the next spiritual plane after they've died. A visitation by a spirit is quite deliberate. If she's with you, it must be out of a desire to help you somehow. Once we shed our mortal flesh, our spirits are largely focused on growth and the desire to aid others in growth. Other considerations just become much less important."

His matter-of-fact delivery startled her a bit. "You sound as if you believe this stuff."

And then his face broke into one of those rare smiles that seemed to transform his features. "Do I strike you as deceptive, Deborah?"

"No, you don't. That way of thinking is different from what I'm used to."

"What about your aunt?"

"My aunt?" she shifted a bit in her chair, not remembering if she'd discussed this aspect of her aunt at any length with him. "She had some unorthodox ideas about herbal remedies and energy. Always protect your energy. But I was never really sure about what she meant."

He was watching her again, studying her in a way that made her a bit uneasy, "Well, she was right about that. On the earthly plane, people fight to gain money and power, but those more aware of the higher stakes of things struggle over a different commodity— energy, as your aunt said."

Smiling, "I would have never pegged you to be so New Age."

"It's nothing new, actually something very, very old."

She felt herself beginning to relax, be less guarded around him, and not feel so much that she needed to be anything but herself. And the attention that he gave her was a bit dizzying. She wasn't used to it, and it was compelling.

"What are we doing?"

"In what sense?"

They'd gotten a coffee and were strolling not far from her house. Night had fallen several hours before, but she didn't feel unsafe with him beside her.

"The dinners, the time we're spending together, I'm just wondering what your goal is."

He laughed softly, "You think I have a goal?"

"I—I'm not sure. Let's say it's something that I feel."

He took her hand in his. "So, tell me more about what you're feeling, Deborah."

She wished dearly now that she hadn't opened her mouth. Why couldn't she just leave it alone? Why did she have to dissect things and be suspicious? "I'm sorry. I shouldn't have said that."

He stopped walking and stared at her. She could see his face illuminated by a nearby streetlamp in the yard they'd just passed. "Don't apologize to me, please. I'd much rather you speak to me honestly."

Taking a breath, it was odd how unsettling he could be at times. "I just sense things. I always have. I guess it's a form of intuition or something. And what's going on between us, this acquaintance, feels different, as though I should understand something I don't."

"You haven't had many relationships, have you, Deborah?" he said softly. She thought she should take offense, but it didn't feel like he meant it that way.

"No, not really."

"Believe me when I say I'm here spending time with you because it's what I want. I am very drawn to you, extremely interested in knowing you, all of you."

And then he bent in closer, kissing her softly in that way that made her heart race. And that nagging feeling that there was more to understand here fled momentarily from her mind.

Escalation

Chapter Ten

"How's Deborah?"

His uncle had texted him late last night that he was in town. And sometime around mid-morning, he'd dropped in at Daniel's Moss St. Address, a modest little cottage well-hidden in an unobtrusive cul-de-sac off Bayou St. John. Being in proximity to the water felt energizing, as well as having a home near an area of town that had been settled early on, predating New Orleans, and quite often inhabited by mystical practitioners.

He handed his Uncle Silas a steaming mug of coffee and settled into a wicker chair across from him. They were sitting out on his screen porch, a roomy space with an ample view of the night sky when indeed, it was nighttime. "She's well. I saw her last night."

"And I take it you have been seeing a lot of her."

He inhaled a bit sharply. Clearly, his uncle wasn't just making small talk. He had something in mind. "I thought you were in Scotland."

"I was, but now I'm back. Have you told her anything?"

He wasn't ready to talk about Deborah Brandt, particularly with a man he viewed as a father figure. At present, he felt very protective about what was happening between them. "Uncle Silas, undeniably, it is a rare treat to have you drop in on my doorstep, but I'm not a teenager, and my relationship with Deborah—"

"Is no ordinary relationship, my boy, you know that. Things are escalating in this city. There are pockets of extremely negative conduits developing."

Sighing, he sipped the hot coffee. He was aware. He would have had to be pretty detached not to notice. "Yes, I know."

"It is believed she could be a powerful ally to help counterbalance this. That you two—"

He put his mug down abruptly on the glass coffee table between them with a clang. "Deborah is not a weapon to be used. She is a lovely human being and has no experience of anything you are describing."

"Then you might need to start teaching her."

"I'm not sure it's fair to bring all of this into her life."

"Is it fair not to my boy? When one isn't walking their path, there is a restlessness, a deep and abiding dissatisfaction with almost everything."

"Yes, I know, but timing is important."

"Of course, but don't let abundant caution turn into fear."

"Have you ever known me to be particularly fearful?"

Smiling at him as he remembered when he was a boy, "You, no, not really, but then again, this relationship is new territory. Can I meet her?"

Retrieving his mug and taking a sip, "Not yet." He wasn't ready. She wasn't ready, not yet.

Last night had been different. After their walk, they'd gone back to her aunt's house. And they'd fallen into that odd routine where he would look around the house a bit, kiss her goodnight, and then leave. But tonight wasn't the same. This night Daniel didn't at all seem in a rush to leave.

He'd sat down on her aunt's sky-blue sofa in the den and held out his hand for her. Deborah hadn't thought much about this relationship, or rather where it might be going, despite questioning him earlier in the evening. There was an unreal quality between them, a strange, insulated feeling that largely left her content as things unfolded from moment to moment. Smiling, she sat beside him, allowing him to take her hand.

"Daniel," she'd murmured just as he'd pulled her more closely in an embrace. Of course, he'd kissed her before, sometimes passionately, sometimes chastely, but this time. This decidedly felt different, dizzying, intense as his lips moved down to her neck and throat. His hands across her back and under her clothes were moving, caressing. She hadn't expected it, although she supposed she should have. They'd been on four, no, maybe five dates now. It wasn't all that surprising that, at this point, intimacy might ensue. But this involvement, if that indeed was what it was, didn't feel like anything ordinary.

His touch was so warm, making her fluid, languorous, even relaxed as he leaned her back into a reclining position on the couch.

Distantly, she wondered how far she would let him go. He was boldly touching her beneath her blouse, kissing her everywhere. And then his hands moved to her pants, running his palms along her legs, her hips. Her breath caught in her throat. He wanted her, wanted her very much. She could feel it intently as though it were her thought. And then the fear cascaded in, the fear that had always protected her. She pulled up a bit, still in his embrace, but putting her hand on his chest, "Daniel, wait."

He stopped, sitting up a bit. His eyes were glazed, she thought, from the intensity of the moment. And she felt her breathing so deep. "I—I'm sorry. I'm just not ready."

He was looking at her so intensely, and then he pulled her against him firmly in his arms. "I'm sorry, Deborah," he whispered to her. "I shouldn't have pushed things so soon."

"No, no, it's all right."

He kissed her softly on the lips again, and she felt that hypnotic haze settle over her. It would be easy, so easy to let him make love to her, and she had regrets in the moment of not doing so. But she wasn't ready. That was simply the truth. As he began to pull away from her, he murmured, "I'm going to go."

She sat up, awkwardly readjusting her clothing as he stood up. "Daniel, I don't want you to think that I'm not interested. I've just always been cautious about this type of—"

"Intimacy?" he filled in, holding his hand out and gently pulling her to her feet.

"Yes," feeling a bit embarrassed. She'd never had this type of conversation with a man, much less anyone. "I'd just like to give things a little more time. That's all."

He was eying her contemplatively, not seeming put off in the least. "Well, I'm not going anywhere, Deborah," he said softly before he pulled her into another close embrace. "But don't doubt how drawn I am to you, how attracted, as long as you understand that."

"I do," she murmured, kissing him again and wondering.

His uncle left his house not long after their conversation. He claimed to have business in the city and would be in contact. Uncle Silas didn't seem particularly put off about Daniel's reluctance to let him meet Deborah. But the truth was that he felt protective of her, of what was happening between them. Last night things had changed between them. He knew if he'd been persistent, he would have slept with her and had to rein in his impulses to stop himself from doing just that. The draw he felt to her was powerful, more so than even he had anticipated, though he had been warned.

He sat down in the rattan rocker on his screen porch, closing his eyes. Mostly, he was trying to clear out the clutter of thoughts that felt insistent on closing in on him. His emotions, while usually well sorted, felt in a muddle. He didn't like to feel as though he were losing his way. His uncle was right. Things were happening here in the city. He could feel it.

He focused on Deborah, seeing her sitting in a classroom, surrounded by other people. Then he allowed his focus to be drawn elsewhere, to her the night before. He could see her asleep in her bedroom upstairs. A window was partially opened, and the drape fluttered in a light breeze. He breathed deeply, feeling that her spirit was traveling as all spirits do in sleep. He allowed his consciousness to follow her and be drawn to where she was.

Dreams

Chapter Eleven

"Pay attention to your dreams."

Someone had told her that. Had it been her aunt? It was difficult to remember. But now she was pulled along, outside, walking. The wind blew around her in a way that felt cold, but it wasn't chilling. It was so dark, but places along the street were illuminated, particularly around the park, the one a few streets away from her house.

She was dressed in her long nightshirt, barefoot, but easily moving from the street into the graveled park. The grounds were lit by a few streetlamps, the only area around that was, while directly above a luminescent half-moon that shone in the night sky.

She breathed deeply in the chilled air, but it didn't bother her. She was part of it somehow.

What does it mean? — a whisper in her mind.

Everything was quiet, deserted, but at the same time alive with movement. The swings were shifting erratically though there was no one there. The seesaw was also active in its up-and-down kinetic motion, completely unoccupied. And the merry-go-round spun rapidly as though hands were continually pushing it, but there was only emptiness everywhere. No one except the crows, crows fluttering their black wings, situated in the monkey bars, on the play gym, the top of the slides, along the steel bar atop the swing set.

This place felt alive, but it wasn't. There was something else. "What does this mean?" She murmured aloud.

"It's important somehow." It was Daniel's voice, speaking to her now. In fact, he was standing next to her as though he'd been there all along.

"Why is everything moving?" As though it was quite natural for her to ask.

"It's energy. There's an energy here."

"But what about the crows?"

"They eat dead things. The negative energy is drawing them. They're not bad, just harbingers. Sin Eaters, if you will."

Sin Eaters? She turned the concept slowly over in her mind. Then abruptly, she felt weak as though something had been drawn out of her. And she felt his arms go around her.

"Come with me. You can't stay here long."

Within the span of a blink, they were somewhere else, somewhere entirely different. His arms were still around her, holding her against him.

"Daniel, where are we?" She could sense water, feel it near, although it was soundless.

"It's all right."

"I'm so tired."

"You were drained."

She could feel his skin against hers as he pushed her onto the bed. She thought to talk but didn't. It felt right, his hands on her, his mouth on hers, and then he was making love to her.

He opened his eyes, breathing in sharply. It was disorienting, traveling like this, particularly navigating the terrain of someone else's dream. He was still on the porch though the sky outside had darkened a bit, probably heading toward an afternoon thunderstorm. He felt shaky. The intensity of the dream had been powerful.

It was true that they had not been together in the flesh. But their spirits had merged, and it had changed things. It was overwhelming in some respects. He hadn't expected this to happen, but in retrospect, he didn't know why he hadn't. It's where they had been headed and still were.

She remembered the birds, black birds all over the place. And there was that vivid sensation of Daniel being there with her and holding her so closely. She stopped walking in the corridor of Monroe Hall at Loyola. Strange, that she didn't remember this from earlier, but in the dream, she could feel him against her, touching her, his skin next to hers — so vivid. And then the feeling when he was actually making love to her, just recalling the memory, took her breath away. She began to walk again. Clearly, it must have been spurred on by what happened last night before he'd gone home.

That was what she told herself. But the truth was that it didn't quite feel that way. The dream left her shaken, tangibly, emotionally shaken, as though something inside her felt quite different. She steeled herself, trying to concentrate on the day ahead of her. Classes in the morning and work in the afternoon. Most likely, she wouldn't see Daniel today. That might be for the best, she supposed, while she sorted all these odd emotions out. After all, it was just a dream. It shouldn't really mean anything.

Attack

Chapter Twelve

It was startling. In fact, startling enough that she almost jumped out of her skin. Deborah was sitting in front of one of the computer terminals in Loyola's Monroe library searching for a source for her latest cyber journalism paper when suddenly she felt a hand on her back, not just on her clothing, but covering enough of the fabric that it touched skin near her neck.

Instinctively, she jolted away and turned sharply to find herself looking into the face of Ross Everton, a tall, muscular, curly-brown-haired fellow who was also a journalism major and someone she'd been acquainted with ever since she'd started at the University. He was smiling widely, laughing at her reaction. "Settle down, bookworm. I just wanted to say hi."

It was odd. She was breathing deeply and still felt shaken, as though she was curiously out of breath. "Yeah, you scared me."

Again, the broad smile, "Evidently, you've got to get out of the caverns once in a while, girl. You're way too skittish."

She shook her head, her focus returning to the computer screen. It would be nice if he just went away now, so she could pull herself together. "Well, I've got a lot to do."

He dragged a small wooden chair next to hers, sitting down, clearly not taking the hint that the intrusion was unwelcome. "Yeah, about that, Debby. I think I have a fix to cure all your ills."

She sighed, staring at the screen. It wasn't that she didn't like Ross. He was a nice enough guy, but right now, his just being beside her felt extremely irritating. "Like I said, I really—"

"I know, but there's a party at Phi Kappa on Saturday. I thought you might like to go with me."

Yep, fraternity stuff. That was one of the reasons she had never considered going out with Ross Everton. He was so deep into the fraternity scene. "Um, thanks, Ross, but I really can't," she muttered, hoping that would be the end of this rather quickly.

"Nope, I'm not going to take no for an answer Debby." And he'd always called her Debby, even when she'd told him not to —another reason she did not want to date him.

"Well, I'm sorry about that, Ross, but I'm afraid you're going to have to."

"Come on, Debby, just one party, and you'll see how charming I can be."

She looked at him and wanted to smile. He was a nice guy, definitely superficial, but he would never be her guy. "I can't. I'm seeing someone, Ross. You know, a boyfriend." The word boyfriend felt uncomfortable somehow, particularly in applying it to Daniel. Whatever they were or were becoming, the labels boyfriend and girlfriend felt strangely inappropriate.

He leaned back in his chair. "You have a boyfriend?" He did look a little stunned. Why was that, exactly?

She attempted to refocus on the screen in front of her. "Yeah, a boyfriend."

"Oh," he said, still looking a bit befuddled, "well okay, then I'll let you get back to it." He stood up, still looking down at her, a bit confused.

She smiled briefly, "Have fun, I mean on Saturday."

He nodded, "Right," seeming curiously deflated as he left. Was it so bizarre to believe that she was in a relationship?

She shook her head, trying to return to the task at hand. But oddly, she still felt it, the physical pressure where he'd touched her. It felt strangely uncomfortable in that spot, particularly on the skin near her neck.

The whole episode was somewhat perplexing. It was true that she always acted separate, outside the periphery of the normal University social life. Maybe that's what he found confusing about her. She'd never tried to be a part of it, any of it because somewhere deep down, she had accepted that she was different.

"How are you?"

"Fine, I guess, maybe a little tired. I'm backed up with school, and I don't seem to have the energy or concentration to handle it."

There was silence for a moment on the line. He was thinking, weighing things. She smiled. She was getting to know Daniel, how he operated. "You know, I have some work to finish as well. I could pick up some Chinese and bring it over to your house. Then I won't interfere with what you need to do."

She considered. Having him here, would it be a help or a major distraction? "You might get bored."

"No, I think I'd like a quiet night. But only if you can get your work done."

"We can give it a try," she said softly, realizing suddenly that she would like to see him.

"Good, I'll be there around six."

She could hear the crows in the morning outside her window, sending out a call to one another. Her mind wandered to where they were, high atop the tall oak trees in her aunt's small backyard.

They rustled restlessly through the well-concealed branches, their black wings brushing against the leaves, the twigs. She could feel their agitation. Something, something was closing in. She closed her eyes, sinking deeper, deeper somewhere.

Clear your mind. She breathed deeply. Was that her thought or someone else?

Again, she breathed in deeply. Her mind traveled back to the graveside, the small ceremony beside the plot where her Aunt Gena's ashes were interred. She wore a black knit dress with a brown belt and brown boots.

"Why did you wear that, Debby? Didn't you have anything else?"

She shifted. That was right. She'd forgotten her mother's comment. It agitated her, prickled her. *You must release the irritations. Let them go as though they are meaningless, or they will anchor you.*

She breathed in deeply, then released it, releasing the upset, letting it part from her. *Good, good.*

She felt herself traveling. Everything changed. Now she was in the hospital, sitting beside her aunt's bed. She was alone. Others would be coming but not yet. Her aunt was still deep in a coma. And the nurses said it could be anytime.

She remembered the upset, the grief. *Let it go. Release it all.*

Again, she let the emotion, the overwhelming sadness, and confusion peel away from her. *Good,* she felt the lightest touch on her shoulder and turned. Her aunt looked down at her smiling. *"Now, you can see."*

The ringing jolted her abruptly awake. She'd briefly sat down in her aunt's rocking chair and must have dozed off. Glancing up at the old cuckoo clock on the wall, she saw it was nearly six. Again, the front doorbell chimed. Her mind was disoriented, still feeling as though she were trapped back in those dreams, or were they flashes of memory, so confusing.

She headed to the front door, running her hands through her hair quickly. She had no idea what she looked like but swung it open.

Daniel was standing there with bags in hand, looking a bit puzzled. "I was beginning to think you weren't in."

"Sorry, I just sat down for a few minutes and fell asleep. I guess I've been pushing too hard lately."

"Do you want to do this another time?" he asked smoothly. Clearly, he was concerned about her. It was odd. It certainly wasn't on his face, but she could feel it acutely on her skin.

"No, no," she opened the door wider. "Come on in, and I'll try to pull it together."

He walked through, smiling, "No need on my account."

She smiled, feeling the fatigue drifting away just being near him.

Chapter Thirteen

He didn't like it. Something was off with Deborah, and he had a fairly good suspicion of what it was. They'd set their work and dinner up on her aunt's cherry wood coffee table. He'd brought his laptop, and Deborah had hers, as well as various books and notebooks. She wasn't talking a great deal and, in truth, seemed abnormally tired.

It bothered him. There were questions he could ask, but then again, it might tip her off to the fact that more was going on here than met the eye. Or worse yet, make her believe he was prying into personal areas of her life.

She looked up from a book, smiling. "I'm sorry. I'm not such great company tonight."

"No, I'm enjoying this, just quietly spending time together. Can I get you a cup of tea?"

Her eyes widened a bit. She had such lovely eyes, deep hazel but mostly green tonight. "That sounds great. There is some green tea in the cabinet in the kitchen, to the right of the stove."

He rose to his feet. "Be right back," he murmured. He'd never been in the kitchen at Deborah's house, but he knew where it was, just past the staircase through an open doorway. It was a galley-style kitchen but much wider, leading to a larger alcove that nestled a breakfast table and large windows looking into the backyard. He opened the long pantry to the right of the stove and spied the tea boxes on the top shelf. Quickly, he came to the green tea, pulling it down, and two blue ceramic mugs hanging on hooks beneath the cabinets.

As he poured water into the cups from a nearby Brita pitcher, he felt things. He could feel her Aunt Gena in this kitchen, moving around, and later her body in pain as she struggled to do daily tasks. He could feel Deborah here — distracted, confused, then lonely and so depressed after her aunt's passing. He placed one mug in the microwave over the stove and punched in the appropriate time. He leaned against the counter, allowing those emotions he was feeling to pass through him. It could be exhausting, entertaining someone else's pain. It was the loneliness that seemed to bother him the most. She'd been so very lonely, even when there were people about. She'd always felt apart, different, intent on hiding herself out of fear, fear that she would be misunderstood, rejected. All of that echoed with an undeniable familiarity within him. Even though he did have a small, supportive circle, in relation to most of the world around him, he'd always felt apart, disconnected from the mainstream. Of course, he'd been taught it was because he had a different calling than most, but that certainly didn't make it any easier.

The microwave beeped, pulling him out of his reflective state. He placed the second mug within and decided to focus, focus on Deborah and who had put their hands on her today.

"You're vulnerable right now."

"Vulnerable? How do you mean?"

He was sixteen, and he and his Uncle Silas were living in Carmel, along the coast of California. Much of his childhood after his mother left had been spent relocating to different parts of the country with his uncle. His early education consisted mainly of personal tutors or short forays in private schools. And in addition, there had been his other education with his uncle, mother, and sometimes others as his guides.

"You're evolving, your abilities, your gifts. Until this process settles down, you need to be wary of problematic places and people."

"People? What sort of people?"

"People intent on draining your energy, consciously or not — right now they'll be drawn to you, sniff out your lack of protection, so to speak. Try not to allow strangers or anyone you are not confident of put their hands on you."

"You mean it's that simple for them."

"Unfortunately, yes."

Daniel let the two steaming cups of tea brew in front of him on the kitchen cabinet and allowed his awareness to grow, to expand. His vision moved back into the den where Deborah was seated on the couch, continuing to make notes from a book. He'd traveled this house many times over, sometimes in his dreams, sometimes in conscious meditation as he was ostensibly doing now. He focused on her and then traveled backward feeling earlier in the day when she wasn't so depleted of energy.

He could see her clearly in another setting. Glancing around, he understood it was a library at the college, and she was sitting in a chair in front of a computer screen. He waited patiently. Surely there was something important to observe here. And then a man, or more of a boy in his estimation, approached her. He grabbed her arm in familiarity and put his hand on her back. Daniel felt a quick surge of jealousy that he hadn't expected. Deborah spun around, seeming alarmed at first, and then her features softened, an acquaintance. But then he felt that sickening feeling when one witnesses another being exploited by a parasite.

"That's ungenerous," his mother had explained to him.

"But that's what they are, no better than insects or other creatures draining the essential life force out of another."

"We all go through that level of evolution at one time or another."

"Why can't they gain their own energy instead of stealing it from someone else?"

"Try to step back, Daniel, and think with detachment."

He tried to dismiss the moment's emotion, his protectiveness of Deborah, and his jealousy that this person felt he had a right to put his hands on her. All of that was not helpful. What was clear was that this person had drained her energy, and what was also clear was that she was vulnerable, perhaps evolving. He brought himself back into the present. Perhaps his contact with her had ignited this stage of development within her, but he had to get her past this vulnerability. There was too much out there just now, eager to take advantage of it.

Quickly, he found the sugar bowl and finished making the tea. She was probably wondering why he was taking so long, and unfortunately, he had few answers to give.

When he returned to the den, he saw immediately that she had leaned against a decorative pillow on the sofa and fallen asleep. He frowned, putting the cups on the coffee table and settling in the rocking chair directly across from the couch. This had hit her so hard. It was no good. It was unacceptable that he had come into her life and then become a detriment to her.

He closed his eyes and began trying to find her.

It was loud where she was, wherever she was. The room was so crowded, people pushing by the table, bumping into her, scraping her skin where it was exposed, at her arms, her neck.

"I need to go," she murmured in confusion.

There was a hand pressing over hers, then yelling into her ear. "You just got here. He'll be here soon."

Again, she looked around at crowded tables, strangers laughing and drinking. That's right, she remembered. Her friend Margo had set her up on a date with —

"There he is, Tom."

Her eyes looked up, and the room seemed smoky. Were people supposed to be smoking in here? Her eyes followed Margo's to the young man walking up to the table, but it wasn't Thomas Stratford as she'd remembered. It was Ross, Ross Everton from the library earlier that afternoon. "Wait a minute, Margo. That's not—"

But then her voice collapsed in her throat. It wasn't Margo anymore. It was her friend Jessica. She was laughing so buoyantly. "I told you he liked you, so I invited him."

Her head swirled. This wasn't what happened, not at all. Ross pulled a chair up next to her at the table that was crowded with people that she didn't know, strangers. "Good to see you again, Debby. Let's take a walk outside."

And then he'd grabbed her forearm, and it burned, burned so much she wanted to scream. She pulled away, "No, stop it. I'm not going." And everyone at the table was looking at her as though she was insane.

Jessica whispered to her hotly. "Don't make a scene, Deborah."

And then she felt someone else grabbing her, pulling her out of Ross's grasp to her feet. Vision swam in front of her, but she knew him, knew Daniel's face.

"Come on," he said with steel in his voice. His arm was around her now as he was pulling her away, away outside the club.

"What is this?" she murmured.

"A bit of a nightmare, I should think," he said flatly.

She breathed in the night air. It felt better, like a cool mist surrounding her. And his arm, his arm behind her back, hand on her arm, was helping, so calming, soothing even.

"Hey, Debby, who is that guy? Come on back inside." It was Ross, Ross yelling behind them."

"Ignore it," Daniel said a bit gruffly.

"What's happening?"

"Don't worry. It will be all right." He stopped walking and then said to her in a determined voice. "Close your eyes, Deborah."

"What?"

"Just do it."

"Why?" she asked, feeling more than uncomfortable just following orders.

"Because we need to travel."

She had no idea what that might mean, but she complied.

When she slowly opened her eyes again, she expected to have returned to Aunt Gena's house, but she wasn't there. She was sitting on a small sofa against a paneled wall in another place. Daniel was right next to her, holding her, softly rubbing her arm, the arm that Ross had grabbed.

She breathed in deeply, feeling warm, comfortingly so, and relaxed as though she could lean against him and then slip into a deep sleep. "Where are we?"

"My house, well, the one by the water."

"I—I don't understand. We were at Aunt Gena's house, then—"

"Then you fell asleep."

"This is a dream?"

"Of a fashion," he murmured. Then he pulled her even closer against the side of his body. "Who was that guy?"

"Guy?"

"Where you were, and from earlier — the one who grabbed your arm."

"Ross, Ross Everton."

"Old boyfriend?" he asked.

"No, he wanted to go out with me, but I said no. Why do—"

"Try to avoid him. He drained your energy. You're vulnerable right now."

"Vulnerable? Why?"

"Your spirit is evolving. It's because we've been spending time together, Deborah. Trust me. Stay away from him, all right."

"Okay, I guess so," she whispered, still tired.

He nodded, "Good," then he pulled her closer to him and started to kiss her, kiss her passionately in a way that made her feel as though she was melting. And she felt his hands on her, all over her, then beneath her clothes, touching and igniting something deep within her.

She jolted awake, feeling his hand lightly touching her arm. "Deborah, I'm sorry."

She straightened up on the couch, sheer dizziness sweeping around her. "It's okay," she said, looking around bleary-eyed. "I'm sorry. Did I fall asleep?"

He smiled, "You seemed exhausted. I put the food in the fridge. I think you should get some rest."

"Oh, okay, sorry, wow, great date, huh?"

He smiled softly, "Always, lock the door behind me."

Daniel put his laptop in the car and sat in the driver's seat for a moment, staring back at the house. One by one, lights began to go off downstairs. Clearly, she was taking his advice. He wondered how much of the dream she would remember. And he wondered if he should simply knock on the door and insist on spending the night with her, with her in her bed. He had no doubt the contact would help her, perhaps help her and him get past this rut that they seemed stuck in. But the timing—and that was what seemed to be stopping him, the timing. Or was it? Was it the concern and, dare he say, fear of crossing that threshold? Because he knew unequivocally that once he did, things would be set in motion.

Deborah was still tired, but it was a restless sort of tiredness. Once Daniel left, she gave up on studying further. There was simply no point. She put on a nightshirt that she usually wore to bed and began to pace her bedroom. She felt peculiar. Things were clinging to her, disconnected images, sensations, memories of being held and touched, but that hadn't happened. Tonight had been a bust. They'd eaten dinner, and sometime after, she'd fallen asleep and dreamed — feverish, disconnected dreams about being held by him, Daniel, so close, so soothing.

And she could still feel his touch on her skin as though it had really happened. But it had just been a dream. With weariness, she flopped onto her bed. This, all of this, was just so confusing and strange. She didn't understand what was happening.

She closed her eyes, trying to clear her mind as her aunt had taught her. "The mind needs attention as much as the body Deborah." Aunt Gena had encouraged her to attempt meditation at least once a day. She sat up in her daybed and crossed her legs with her palms face up on her lap. "Let everything go, all thoughts, all concerns, just let it drift." It was almost as though she could hear her voice in her mind. She breathed deeply, trying to relax and drift.

"Now, do let go," there was a whisper, not her aunt's voice, but someone else, coaxing her.

What happened next was hard to describe because she genuinely didn't understand it. But she felt drawn away, drawn away to another place.

"Do you speak to her?"

"Her—" she repeated the word.

"Your mother?"

"Oh," she murmured. It wasn't clear. In fact, nothing was clear. "No, not often."

"Why?" It was a woman's voice, quizzing her. That much had solidified, the gender, but not much else.

"She doesn't think of me often."

There was quiet, not an immediate response. She didn't know why she'd said exactly that. The usual response would be that she was busy, wrapped up in her life, her new family. They'd drifted apart. But this response, well, some would think it harsh.

"*I see,*" was the reply.

"Why?"

"*Yes.*"

"Why did you ask that?"

"*I was wondering why you seem on your own so much.*"

She considered. "Am I?"

"*Some, of course. You do have Daniel now. You can be part of his family if you wish it.*"

"I—I don't know if that's true."

"*You need each other. Don't fight it, my dear. Things are only getting more difficult.*"

She opened her eyes. It was her room. She was back in her room, nowhere else. A breeze fluttered the gauzy shears that covered her opened window. "*Sleep now.*" It was a mere whisper from somewhere, perhaps in her mind. But she closed her eyes, allowing the fatigue to sweep over her.

The Gallery

Chapter Fourteen

"Are you working this weekend?"

"No, I scheduled off Saturday. I've just been tired lately. I thought I could use a break."

She'd woken this morning feeling so out of sorts. She'd even taken out a notebook and attempted to write down the flashes of memory from her dreams the night before. The recollections were broken but vivid in some ways, walking outside the bar with Daniel, what happened inside, the confusion, then being somewhere else with him, another house — and of course, her aunt's voice and the other, the woman talking to her. That still unidentified presence had been strangely comforting, not just the content of what was said, but the presence itself felt so calming.

"That's good. You need some rest, though I thought I'd like you to come to my house. I'm actually not a terrible cook." *Of course, you do have Daniel now. You can be part of his family if you wish it.* She remembered now, remembered the woman's words from the dream.

"Oh," feeling a little caught off guard, he did tend to do that to her. "I have class today and work this afternoon. But the weekend would be fine."

"Saturday?"

"Okay, do you want me to meet you there?"

"No, I'll pick you up."

It was after one when she arrived at the Sauveterre Gallery. It was a Friday afternoon, and the French Quarter was already beginning to amass its weekend visitors. She usually dismissed its busy population without a second thought, but today it bothered her, in fact, more than bothered her. It was distinctly on her skin, a heaviness, irritation, like a light film of sweat. And uncharacteristically, even entering the gallery's heavy mahogany and glass doors today felt a bit daunting, an undeniable dread in the pit of her stomach, so strong and yet intangible.

At about three o'clock, Colleen Marsh passed by her desk, admittedly looking as distracted as Deborah felt. Today, the time had been dragging torturously slow. She had tried to focus on some reading for school, which had evolved into a ridiculously fruitless task.

"Plans tonight, Deborah?" Colleen murmured off-handedly as she rifled through a stack of papers she'd brought and abruptly plopped down on the reception desk. Deborah wondered what had prompted her to do so, as her office was more than roomy enough to accommodate her. But then again, maybe Colleen, on some level, was desperate for human interaction. In heavy contrast to the busy Quarter outside, this place had been a virtual ghost town all day.

"Tonight? No, not really, you?"

She smiled a bit grimly, and Deborah noted that this seemed to be a default position on Colleen's slim and bony face. "Yes, dinner plans, an old friend from up North."

Deborah nodded, not inquiring further. The truth was she didn't want to know. Mr. Segretti had intimated, in his not-too-subtle manner, that Colleen Marsh was a lesbian, engaging in an on-again-off-again romance with a music professor from Connecticut of all places, not that Deborah cared. Everyone's business was just that, their business. In response, she smiled, saying nothing. She'd cultivated a non-gossipy demeanor as she didn't want her private life perused too closely by anyone at the gallery. "Sounds nice."

Colleen glanced up at her from her stack of papers as though something she'd said had caught her interest. "Pretty girl like you must have some fellow interested."

So strange how the comment unnerved her, and it really shouldn't. She'd known Colleen for years. But something about the way her sharp brown eyes were looking at Deborah sent a warning shot right up her spine. And she didn't for a moment think it was a romantic interest. That she could spot easily.

Something was just off. She leaned back in her chair, retaining her calm, professional attitude. "Well, I like to keep things simple." She was determined. Her private life would stay just that, private.

Colleen gave her that odd sort of slanted smile of hers that she had always felt to be laced with a strong dose of sarcasm. "Good girl." Then she picked up her papers and left as abruptly as she'd arrived. Deborah nervously glanced down at her watch; only two hours to get through, then she could leave. She took a deep breath inward, but it felt difficult, heavy to her, as though it pained her chest to draw it in. Perhaps a doctor's visit soon, a check-up, but deep down, she felt sure it wasn't physical. Aunt Gena would, and then she stopped herself. Damn, that hurt. It had been some time since she'd made that mistake, forgetting that she was gone, forgetting that she wouldn't be there when she had some problem to ask about.

She closed her eyes, trying to clear her mind. And wondered distractedly why she really didn't want anyone at the gallery to know about Daniel, to know that she'd been seeing him.

She remembered the woman's voice last night — *You can be part of his family if you wish.* Was that indeed what she wanted? She picked up her cell phone, glancing down. She thought about how comforting he was to her and instinctively began to text.

Are you busy? Without much thought, she'd sent it quickly.

In mere moments, there was a reply. **No, is everything all right?**

She swallowed. What in the world did she want to say? This felt awkward. She'd never texted him before. They'd always spoken on the phone. **Nothing is wrong. I am at work. Things are slow here.** Coward, that wasn't what she wanted to say. She wanted to tell him what she would have told Aunt Gena.

Are you all right, Deb?

She smiled. He'd called her Deb. She wasn't sure if he'd done that before, but she liked it. At least, for some reason, she liked him doing it. **Yeah, the Quarter just seems strange today.**

Without missing a beat, **Strange, how?**

She took a breath. They'd talked about this before — energy, impressions. Undeniably, he was open to her feelings about things. **I know it will sound odd, but there seems to be a heaviness, denseness, difficult to breathe as though the air is thick.**

Within only seconds, **What time are you off?**

Five

I'll meet you outside.

Her heart started pounding. She hadn't intended this, but somehow it buoyed her spirits. **I have my car.**

I'll take an Uber.

Are you sure?

Yes, of course.

Okay, she said, because she felt overwhelmed, gratified even, and she didn't quite know how to express it.

"Why are you so insecure?"

"I'm not."

Aunt Gena frowned as she eyed her critically. Or at least it felt critical to Deborah. "You second-guess every decision you make."

She laughed, feeling pain inside as the comment hit too close to the truth. "That's not true."

"My dear, don't lie to yourself. There's no point, nothing to gain there. After all, you don't want to alienate the only person who will always be on your side."

That advice filtered in as she sat at the receptionist desk at the Sauveterre Gallery. She was counting down the minutes until closing while tortuously second-guessing her decision to contact Daniel just because she had the heebie jeebies.

She took another painful breath, wondering again if she was getting sick, but not really believing that. "Don't ignore your feelings, little one. Don't disregard or bury them. Sometimes they are the only thing protecting you."

She glanced around at the empty showroom. Colleen and Mr. Segretti were ensconced in her office, going over some last-minute business. Even this room felt different now, shadowed, curiously ominous in a way it didn't usually feel. She closed her eyes for a moment, and rather quickly, she began to hear fluttering around her, almost like the cascading of heavy wings brushing across the ceiling. It was a warning, she thought abstractly, as she heard the door chime to announce a visitor. She opened her eyes, looking toward the entrance, but noted no one was there. Standing up, she walked shakily across the shiny black and white mosaic-polished floor to the French doors, which remained motionless. It was strange, nothing here, but something must have triggered the electronic sensor.

Abruptly, a chill slipped over her, accompanied by a nauseating wave of dizziness. As she squinted her eyes, she could see dark, convoluted shadows crawling up the pale white walls of the gallery, stretching out and covering everything in a pale dingy gray as though it had been splattered with something caustic. She squinted her eyes closed again, feeling tangibly ill, trying desperately to clear her mind. This was crazy. It was so difficult to think coherently, get past the fear. Her mind felt tangibly muddled, unable to concentrate. It was so confusing. She had no idea what was happening.

She forced herself to focus, desperately trying to block this madness. As she walked back over to her desk on shaky legs, the sickness she felt inside only intensified. Her hands trembled as she braced them on the cherrywood surface to steady herself against another intense wave of dizziness. Then suddenly, she felt hands go around her waist. Instinctively, she jumped with a jolt of fear.

"It's all right Deborah. It's me," he whispered.

She straightened up, turned around, and looked into Daniel's face. "The door didn't chime. When did you?"

And then she was jolted again by the voice of Mr. Segretti approaching with Colleen from across the room. "Mr. Wren, I had no idea you were so well acquainted with our Miss Brandt." Deborah stiffened in his embrace, and Daniel removed his hands from steadying her.

Horribly awkward in front of her boss and debilitatingly sick at the same moment, what more could a girl ask for? Daniel answered with composure, for which she was grateful. "Hello, Cesaire," he said lightly. "Yes, Deborah and I have been spending some time together."

Colleen's sharp eyes canvassed Deborah knowingly as she extended her hand to Daniel. "Colleen Marsh."

He quickly returned the handshake, then broke contact rather quickly. His focus returned to Deborah as he said softly, "Are you all right?"

"Yes, just a little dizzy, probably hungry," she whispered shakily.

"Ah well, go along, Miss Brandt. Colleen and I will finish closing the gallery." Mr. Segretti said with his customary flourish, seeming content with the turn of events.

Deborah smiled at him, then met the steely eyes of Colleen Marsh, which not so subtly accused Deborah of lying to her.

"I'm sorry to have dragged you out like this."

He didn't answer. He'd said very little since he'd arrived at the gallery except expertly extricating them from a potentially sticky encounter with Mr. Segretti and Colleen. Though, Mr. Segretti did show great deference to Daniel as he had recently made a rather expensive purchase from the gallery. And Colleen, well, she was Colleen.

Very abruptly, he'd asked her to direct him to her car once they left the gallery. And when they'd reached the garage down the street where she parked, he had insisted on driving. This she didn't argue as her head was still spinning from the inexplicable dizziness.

"You didn't tell them we were seeing each other."

"No," she murmured, slumping down in the seat. "I like to keep my personal life away from work. But I guess the cat's out of the bag now."

"Is that a problem?"

"No, at least I don't think so." She breathed in deeply, and again it felt difficult. "I don't know what's wrong with me. I'm feeling so sick."

"Let's get out of this area. It might help. Something very problematic is around today."

She nodded as she felt profound fatigue overtake her.

It was the park again near her house. And it felt cold, so cold here. The crows were everywhere, gathered on the tops of the swing set and the gymnasium, fluttering their great black wings, lulling her, drawing her. She jolted awake.

Daniel was shaking her arm. "You're too weak, Deb, likely to travel places you shouldn't. Stay awake for now."

The French Quarter was inundated with bad energy today. That was the first thing he'd noted as his Uber driver began heading into the city's heart.

The moment Deborah had begun texting him, he knew something was wrong. In just that simple contact from her, he could feel the energy behind it, the agitation, the frantic sort of suppressed fear. It had become easier for him to read her — the closer they'd become, the more time they spent together. But perhaps he'd fooled himself for a while and relaxed, let himself believe that things were simpler than they could ever be.

Once they arrived at Deborah's house, his mind began to sift through things and strategize quickly. Something or someone had gotten to her. She was significantly drained of energy and leaving her alone now was simply not an option.

She'd sat down on the sofa, bending over a bit and rubbing her head. "I feel so strange, so dizzy. I don't understand it. Do you think I need a doctor?"

He sat next to her, taking her hand in his. "No, the first thing I think you need is a shower."

She straightened up, looking at him oddly, "A shower?"

"Yes, it's hard to explain, but it will help."

But then, she was eying him curiously as though trying to see something he was concealing, and as it was, he was concealing much. "Because of energy?"

He was silent. It was a bit of a tightrope, one that felt acutely in the moment as though it was unraveling. "Yes, to get rid of negative energy."

"That's what Aunt Gena would say."

"Well, then clearly, she was a wise woman."

"Yes, okay, what will you do?"

He squeezed her hand softly. "I'll wait for you."

He sat back on Deborah's couch, hearing the shower upstairs. Closing his eyes, he cleared his mind, trying to quell the quixotic panic that had risen in his chest once he'd felt her vulnerability. Perhaps, it was his fault, all of it. Perhaps, it would have been better to stay out of her life.

"Nonsense."

The word floated in from places unknown, and he knew that he was not alone. So, he opened, opened to the guidance because the hard truth was that he had no idea where to go next.

So, that was precisely the question he asked, "What next?"

"Seems as though the next step since you have set upon this path is to make her stronger as quickly as possible. She is growing more sensitive by association, but it's slow and uneven progress."

"She, she doesn't know who I am," he murmured.

"She knows you are important to her. You have opted to cultivate this association as a relationship. So, follow that thread, solidify the relationship."

"But I'm concerned when she knows more, she might," then he stopped. Because the words he was going to use were—she might hate me.

"Daniel, by coming into her life, you have opened a door. Now it's time to walk through and find what is on the other side."

It helped, but then it always had. When Aunt Gena had told her to take a shower and wash off the bad energy that was clinging to her, it had helped. But as she rubbed her skin roughly with the fluffy pink towel she'd taken from the bathroom closet, she reflected that it wasn't her aunt who had directed her to do this. It was Daniel, Daniel Wren, who was sitting downstairs waiting for her. How did he—and then she thought back to other peculiar conversations they'd had about her impressions of things, his life, which he'd been somewhat circumspect about.

She dressed slowly, trying to get her bearings, then methodically dried her hair with the hair dryer while focusing. He talked about energy as her aunt had done, a strange coincidence. She'd run across quite a few people in her twenty-five years of life, and they were the only two she could remember talking about energy this way. Then again, was it? Perhaps many people knew about these things, though not in her circle, and her aunt wasn't so unique. She considered this, but it didn't fit too well amongst the other things, the impressions — the profound draw she felt to this man she couldn't remember ever having felt before.

She checked her reflection in the mirror over her dresser. She was pale, her face a bit pinched looking, no make-up. Perhaps, they'd just say goodnight, and she'd rest, rest and try to sort things out — perhaps.

She made her way downstairs. He was staring through the front window near the door. The drapes were partially open, something she hadn't done. She usually left them closed before she went to work. "I hope I wasn't too long," she said softly.

He turned around, eying her with a warm smile. This she hadn't expected. He'd been so stoic on the drive here. "Are you feeling any better?"

"Yes, actually the shower helped, just a little tired."

"Well then, prepare yourself because I have an idea, a restful one though."

"Okay," she said quietly, taken a little off guard by his sudden enthusiasm.

"I'd like you to come and spend the weekend at my house."

She stood there momentarily, looking at him with a rather stunned expression crossing her face. "What? I mean — I don't understand."

A smile crossed his face, but not like the other one that somehow, she felt was a bit calculated. This one was genuine, amusement perhaps at her flushed incoherence. "Sorry, didn't mean to shock you." And then he moved toward her, taking her hands warmly in his, to comfort, she supposed, or perhaps to influence. That elusive thought had filtered in. When had she become so suspicious? "The truth is I'm worried about you, Deb." Deb again, and when had that become a thing? "I want you to get some rest, and I'd like to take care of you for a bit, just a few days. Look, I have a guest room for you, so you can be comfortable that I have no untoward motives." She smiled, staring into his warm brown eyes filled with light at the moment, and she realized she was suspicious. Something about tonight, his quick action, the way she was feeling at the gallery, had ignited an awareness in her. Untoward motives? The question was what exactly were they and why.

She hesitated. It was quite a leap, but then again, maybe being in his space might help her unravel answers to all these questions floating about. Impulsively, she decided, because in truth she really didn't want to say no. "All right, a few days of rest, that does sound good."

He smiled, and curiously she felt, rather than saw, a tangible note of relief in him, felt it acutely. He'd been concerned, more than concerned that she wouldn't agree. And why had she? Because something was going on, something to do with Aunt Gena, Daniel Wren, and her, more than anything her. "You might want to pack a few things and bring any schoolwork you have. I promise I'll give you as much space as you need."

"All right, just give me a few minutes, Daniel."

She started to pull away, suddenly realizing he was still holding her hands. But then he bent toward her, softly touching his lips to hers. "You've made me very happy," he whispered. Lightly, she pulled back because she didn't want him to see the blush that was beginning to spread across her cheeks.

Daniel's Place

Chapter Fifteen

They had to take her car. And that worked out well because Daniel had assumed that he was driving. And it was important that he did because even though the shower had helped, Deborah still felt like her insides were quivering. Something had happened at the gallery, something that she didn't understand had shaken her deeply, profoundly. Perhaps that was ultimately why she'd decided to go with him. His presence, his calmness, strengthened her in a way that was difficult to explain. The truth was that Daniel was anchoring her during a very confusing time of her life, and she was grateful for his presence, more so than she had acknowledged until now. She'd quickly packed a bag with a few changes of clothes and bath items, make-up, and another with her computer and schoolbooks. And as she did, Deborah didn't bother to ask herself what she was thinking, what she was doing. She hadn't known Daniel Wren all that long, weeks, perhaps a month. And there was so much that she didn't know. She'd hesitated momentarily, hovering over the canvas bag housing her laptop, and sank onto the bed.

Doubts crept in. So fast, everything was happening so fast. She closed her eyes, clearing her mind and reaching out, reaching out and asking for a sign — some sort of sign that she was traveling the right way, because she knew deep down that regardless of what she didn't understand or didn't know about the man downstairs that she did trust him. Naivete or not, she did trust him.

She breathed in and out deeply, mindfully. She remembered Aunt Gena's coaching to allow all thoughts to float away from her and find calm within herself.

She opened herself to guidance.

A familiar feeling settled over her, one of comfort, one that gave her a lightness of spirit. She smiled, hearing the sweet echoes of her aunt's voice, "Follow your heart, my Deborah. Trust yourself and always follow your heart."

"Are you all right?" he asked, squeezing her hand softly. She'd been so quiet since they'd left her house. And more than that, he could feel her focus somewhere else, a million miles away.

She turned from looking out the window of the car back towards him. "Yes, tired, I guess."

"I can make us something to eat when we get to the house, or if you're hungry now, we can stop—"

"No, that's all right. I can wait," she said with distraction.

He didn't like it, her tone. It seemed so distant. And he questioned if he was making the right call here. But forward, forward was the only way to go, he assured himself.

"Is it far?"

"No, it's not a big place, just a sort of cottage tucked along the bayou."

"That sounds nice."

He smiled, "Well, it suits me."

It's very difficult to understand the difference as if you have been holding your breath and can suddenly relax and breathe again freely. The only problem is when you realize you had no idea you'd been holding your breath.

He'd pulled Deborah's car into a shell-graveled driveway along the side of his cottage, just next to his jeep. It was a private cul-de-sac drive just off the main road near Bayou St. John. She straightened up in her seat, staring at the screen porch leading into the small bungalow house, quaint, a light blue color. Again, it wasn't the house at all, but the feeling, a feeling of privacy, being removed, of protection. Daniel touched her arm, and she nearly jumped. She had been so profoundly wrapped up in her impressions.

"It's all right," he murmured.

And she wondered. Was it? Was it indeed?

"You must be hungry." She sat down on the single twin bed facing the partially open window. Its light drapes were fluttering in the breeze.

"Brave to leave windows open in New Orleans," she murmured, realizing distractedly that she did the same thing in her bedroom.

He placed her two bags on a wooden trunk at the foot of the bed. "Actually, I've found this area to be pretty safe. How would you like an omelet?"

She looked up, feeling a bit dazed. It was light in here, all light. Clearly, the room had once been paneled, but that had been painted over with off-white paint. The bedspread was a fluffy, off-white, and blue-stripe comforter, and the furniture a pale wood, with an almost distressed appearance, beneath varying creamy shades. The bed frame was a minimalistic ironwork, dark gray. But everything else was in a soft variation — white, off-white, cream, or the lightest of pastels. Overall, the total effect was one of calming, soothing. "That sounds perfect. Do you need help?"

"No, I can get it. I'll let you get settled. Then you can join me in the kitchen."

Continuing to look around, she commented, "This is really a lovely room."

"Yeah, well, I tried to keep things simple here, for guests, mostly."

"Many guests?"

He shrugged, "Only occasionally, my uncle was here last week. He tends to drop in unexpectedly."

She smiled, feeling that familiar tug for the aunt she'd lost. "Sounds nice."

He looked at her strangely for a moment as though her words impacted him in some way that she'd found indiscernible. "Well, I'll get dinner together," and then he was gone.

She glanced around. What was she feeling? She sighed deeply, closing her eyes, then sensing the pull of the water of the Bayou St. John, just a quick walk from his home. Of course, the water, and then she recognized the energy. And she knew that was why he'd chosen this house.

She leaned back, letting herself lay across the bed. She was so weary, as though she could just fall asleep. Finally, she was relaxing, unaware of how tense she'd been. She breathed deeply, knowing how easy it would be to float away. And then she felt him, in the kitchen, beginning to cook. She sat up abruptly. So strange, she had tangibly felt his presence across the house as though he was standing just next to her. What was this? Was she losing it?

She stood up, checking her appearance in the mirror atop the distressed light wooded furniture. She grabbed her purse to pull out a hairbrush. Bedraggled, that was the best description she could come up with. She brushed out her shoulder-length hair that was still damp in places from her shower. She hadn't even bothered to put on make-up. Everything had happened so quickly.

And then she heard a voice whisper, *Calm*, perhaps on the breeze, perhaps in her head.

And she suddenly just stopped worrying. Without thought, she left the brush on the dresser and headed toward the kitchen.

He didn't have a plan. And he had no idea if that was a good or unbelievably bad thing. He methodically chopped vegetables on the counter, allowing his mind to wander. He could feel her restlessness, feel confusion in her. Part of it was valid, but most seemed like a by-product of the draining. Lack of energy causes anxiety, panic, uncontrolled emotions, and clouds thinking. He'd sensed all of this in her when he'd found her at the gallery. So, he did the only thing he could think of — scooped her up and brought her to his home.

Momentarily, he stopped chopping mushrooms, trying to collect himself. He didn't consider or think it through, just decided that he needed to protect and help her. That wasn't like him. He was a planner, one who most often weighed things carefully, and considered consequences. But today, he'd done none of that.

"Daniel," he was jarred out of his deep thought at the sound of his name.

He turned around slowly. Deborah stood quietly in the doorway staring at him. Eyes wide, face pale — the only way he could describe as vulnerable. He placed the chopping knife down on the counter and crossed the kitchen, quickly, without thought, taking her into his arms.

"It's all right," he murmured, pulling her close against him.

She didn't answer, just allowed him to draw her securely against his body.

It would be impossible to explain to someone who had never experienced such a thing. In a world that seems so intent on judging and labeling, a moment like this would be misinterpreted, miscategorized, and perhaps sorely misunderstood.

It wasn't as if Deborah felt swept away by her emotions or caught up in the moment. She felt as though something deep inside her and more profound than anything she had experience of take hold.

There was no thought, just complete and unerring need. In a world that had divorced itself from spirit, this was spirit manifesting.

Daniel's arms were wrapped tightly around her, their bodies flush against each other, and she felt strength from him, powerful strength flooding into her panicked shell. She reached up instinctively, bringing her mouth to his, and felt him tremble at the desperate contact. The word surrender cascaded through her mind.

She heard him murmur her name against a storm of passionate kissing, but it didn't connect with her. She didn't feel like herself, the woman who had been named and walked this earth in her body. She felt like something and someone else entirely.

His hands moved somewhat frantically over her clothes, and she reached out as well, touching clothing, then skin, feeling the spark of flesh against flesh that blotted out thought.

He stepped back, grasping her arm, pulling her without finesse out of the kitchen, and hurriedly into another room. Outside of murmuring, "Deb," he hadn't spoken. He closed the door behind them, and she saw the double bed, a room she hadn't seen before.

She hesitated momentarily and remembered who she was and what she used to believe. His arms were around her waist from behind, and he whispered in her ear. "Are you sure?"

She breathed in deeply, hearing that drumming in her ears. That moment of answering seemed to have passed as he'd pulled her sweater over her head and was touching her again. His mouth on her back and his hands on her skin, that moment of decision, crystallized thought had passed. Quite smoothly, he turned her around, then scooped her up in his arms and carried her to the bed.

"Deborah, you're going to have to live your life differently."

Her eyes flickered open, taking in the darkness of the night from the window on the far wall of the room. Lights from streetlamps filtered in, lightly illuminating the shadows.

It registered dimly that he must have turned off the lamps while she slept because before, the room was dimly lit. Daniel was sound asleep beside her, the chenille bedspread pulled over him, over his naked body.

Her cheeks burned a bit at that recognition. She was a novice here, in uncharted territory. She breathed in, remembering the profound intimacy and the hunger for each other that she'd felt in herself and him. Once that match was lit, there was no going back. It had been beyond intense, and as she shifted beneath the covers, the soreness between her legs attested to the fact that everything had changed. She sighed deeply as her aunt's words filtered in. "You're going to have to live your life differently."

Was that true?

And if so, what had she done? She stared upward at the brass ceiling fan spinning over Daniel's bed. She felt his light touch brushing her hair away from her eyes. And she looked over at him, watching her.

She hadn't felt him move. He was lying on his side now. "No regrets I hope," he murmured.

She smiled, "No, of course not," disregarding the concerns she'd been toying with only moments before.

There were things to be considered. Ramifications, perhaps change afoot, but he didn't want to contemplate any of that just now. Deborah was asleep when he slipped out of bed, grabbed a robe, and headed to the kitchen.

He moved silently through the darkened house. The clock on the stove told him that it was approaching midnight. They'd been together for hours, in each other's arms, making love, sleeping, waking up, then making love again. It occurred to him now that he'd never fixed them dinner, but he wasn't hungry. His mind, his senses were whirling. He sat on a stool at the bar leading into the kitchen, sipping a glass of water. He hadn't expected this, not exactly, when he'd invited her to stay the weekend. That he'd done out of concern, though somewhere at the back of his mind, he had to admit that he had considered it. But not like this, not this nearly cataclysmic coupling.

He concentrated, steadying himself, feeling acutely as though he'd passed through a raging storm. It was a heady thing to be stripped of one's control, to have your emotions laid bare, to be, in some respects, remade.

Just sex?

He rather doubted that what happened and would no doubt happen again between he and Deborah could ever be labeled as just sex.

He breathed in and out, deliberately trying to allow the energy that they'd created to settle. Of course, he understood how important and transforming what had occurred between them was. But she hadn't been trained as he had been all his life. How exactly would she react to this once the dust settled?

When she'd woken up that morning, she was alone in the bed — Daniel's bed. She looked around, having no idea what time it was. She pulled the covers up more tightly around her. She was cold. Well, of course, she was cold. She was entirely naked beneath the sheets.

Her head throbbed a bit with hunger. After all, they hadn't eaten dinner the night before. Her cheeks flamed a bit at the memory. They'd been occupied, rather passionately occupied. She tried to recall the layout of the house and where exactly her "guest" bedroom was so she could get some clothes when she noticed her robe lying across a chair next to the bed, her robe. That meant he'd gone into her things to get it for her. She sighed a bit, reaching for it. On the one hand, it was a very considerate thing to do given the circumstances, and on the other, it was a bit of an invasion. But given what had happened last night, boundaries seemed a bit blurred.

She decided she wouldn't think about it too much. She also wouldn't think about what this day would be like, what kind of footing she was now on with Daniel if any. She knew many people who would consider last night to be nothing more than another activity, nothing extraordinary. But she was trying to quell the emotional upheaval threatening to overtake her. Things had changed. Everything had changed, though exactly how she couldn't yet articulate.

She slowly got out of bed and reached for the dark purple velour robe. It had been a gift from her Aunt Gena the Christmas before last. As she glanced back at the unmade bed, she flushed at the intense recollections from the night before, reminding her that she was no longer a virgin and doubly that there had been no birth control. "You'll have to live your life differently." Aunt Gena's words ricocheted about in her mind. Had she messed up here? But it didn't feel that way, though it did all feel confusing, the ground shifting more than a bit beneath her feet. She pulled the robe more tightly around her. She would find her room and get dressed, small steps. But just at that moment, Daniel walked through the door, his eyes sweeping over her in a lovely way that made her want to blush again.

"You're up," he said.

"Yes, I'm up," she said, again that crazy unsettling feeling as though everything was insubstantial.

He paused for a moment, staring at her. Now, this wasn't awkward. "I was letting you sleep." He was dressed already in a black t-shirt and faded blue jeans, more casual than she'd remembered seeing him before.

She smiled, "Yeah, is it late?"

"No, not terribly, just after nine." He moved closer, taking her hand in his. Warm, his grip was warm and steadying. "So, how are you feeling?" he murmured.

"Oh, I'm okay," she said a little breathlessly. "I just wanted—"

But he'd cut her off, leaning in and softly kissing her. "Last night was wonderful, Deborah," he whispered, "incredibly special to me."

"Me too," she answered, shakily against his lips. "I—I was going to get dressed, but—"

"But?"

"But I can't remember where the guest room is."

He smiled, pulling her lightly but securely into his arms. "House isn't that big."

"Yeah, but—"

Again, he took her hand, guiding her to the door. "I'll show you, then fix us some breakfast. Do you want coffee?"

"Yes, please," because coffee would clear the cobwebs, at least, she hoped it would.

She'd pulled on a light blue sweater and dark blue jeans, then brushed her hair out, pulling it up into a loose sort of ponytail. When Deborah found him, Daniel was already cooking in the kitchen. Apparently, she was going to get that omelet that she'd been promised last night. "So, a teaspoon of sugar and a little milk?"

She was perched on a stool at the kitchen counter, watching him pour her coffee from the other side. "That's it," she was trying to remember how he knew how she liked her coffee, then she recalled their visit to the Café Du Monde one evening and a few other coffee shops. He must have been paying attention. He placed a steaming ceramic blue mug in front of her.

"Breakfast is almost ready," he said with a quick smile. She nodded, sipping her coffee. Well, he seemed chipper this morning. No reason he shouldn't be, she thought with a curious level of bemusement. How in the world would she avoid the inclination to blush every few seconds? Had that really been her last night — so passionate, so intense? It felt so far removed from the image she'd held of herself, somewhat inept, somewhat awkward, not someone who felt such desire, who felt themselves to be so desirable.

He placed a plate in front of her on the counter and sat beside her, laying down his plate and coffee. "Sorry, I didn't ask you how you liked your omelet. I just sort of put everything in it."

"It looks good," she said. And it did, exploding with cheese, mushrooms, and various vegetables.

And the first bite confirmed her assessment and reminded her of how hungry she was. "Oh, this is great."

He laughed, sipping his coffee. "Well, glad you approve. I usually just cook for myself, so it's good to get another opinion."

She relaxed a bit. Why worry about anything, just enjoy the moment — she thought to herself. And it was that, a lovely moment.

Choices

Chapter Sixteen

There was a cozy little screen porch off the back of Daniel's house where Deborah settled in with her laptop and schoolbooks, trying to finish some of her assignments. She still felt groggy from the night before, but after two cups of praline coffee was determined to forge forward.

As promised, Daniel had found a lovely little nook for her and then gave her the space she needed to work. They hadn't revisited or even discussed the night before, during, or after breakfast. And she wondered if that was how this would be handled, the avoidance game, but she suspected not. He didn't seem to be the type of man to dodge complicated conversations. Maybe he was just letting things settle a bit, letting her adjust before they examined this new tier of their relationship.

She flipped through a journalism textbook with no semblance of concentration. New tier, new complications — what happens next?

Abruptly, she snapped the textbook closed on her lap. This was ridiculous. At this rate, she would be too distracted to get anything done at all. She needed to find a way to get hold and focus. She placed the book on the small glass coffee table in front of the wicker loveseat where she sat.

Breathing, focus on breathing — she remembered Aunt Gena's instructions on meditation, a way to collect one's thoughts. She curled up on the short sofa in a sort of sitting position. "It's essential you be comfortable, Deborah, or your focus will be too much on your body and not allow your mind to clear." It was amazing how definitively she could hear her aunt's voice in her mind as if she were right next to her, coaching her along.

Breathe in, expand. Breathe out, contract. She allowed every other thought and concern to slowly slip away as she only concentrated on these two elemental things, breathing in and out. Breathing in fresh, energizing air and expelling old fears, concerns, things she had no space for — old energy.

This became her complete focus, just concentrating on breathing, but not a restrictive focus, one that was open, one that allowed the flow of new energies into her system. It felt like a sort of dizziness but not a sickening or disabling one. It was a swirl around her and within as though she was lifting off the couch while she knew without question her body remained still — a fluttering feeling, one that she had felt before but not as strong.

Decide.

Something, or was it someone, was gently whispering in her mind, guiding her to some sort of end that seemed confusing.

Focus — was the following command. She continued breathing. It anchored her as the floating, fluttering feeling increased.

It crystallized in her mind, Aunt Gena speaking to her softly about how the spirit leaves the body and travels at night. "This can also happen in waking hours. We are connected to so many levels of existence and consciousnesses that we are not actively aware of." Had they had this conversation? Or were they having it now?

And what would happen if one could actively become cognizant of it?

Decide. Focus.

The directions floated in but stronger this time. What could happen?

Her mind now felt largely like an emptied, blank canvas, then the feeling of Daniel entered so intense that her one pure thought became to find him.

At first, it only felt like a gentle tug, pulling at her, then increasingly stronger. She was not floating anymore. She moved quickly, decisively to another place.

Almost instantly, it crystallized, a bird's eye view of him from the ceiling of a room. It was a place she hadn't seen before, a smaller room filled with light from an open window.

He was sitting behind a light wood-colored desk, maybe pine or cypress, and surrounding him were bookshelves against the walls of the same pale wood filled with ornaments — chunks of crystals, candles, and other odd items. In addition to pictures, she could see several silver swords that hung on the walls.

The pure surge of energy that she felt in the room startled her, and she knew it was designed for just that — energy. It was powerful and disorienting. *Focus, anchor*, was the murmur. There was no doubt now that she was being aggressively guided in this endeavor.

She relaxed her control further, feeling a curious tugging. Daniel appeared focused on his computer, but he suddenly looked forward, then slowly closed the laptop lid. It jolted her, the surprise almost pulling her back to her body, but she resisted. There was something here nagging at her. She concentrated on him, feeling something tangible about him, almost like a dense sort of mist surrounding him. It felt acutely like a strange, distorted layer of energy between them.

Be certain you want to see. Whoever it was cautioned. What did that mean, see? See what?

She focused on Daniel again. She saw him closing his eyes and felt him zeroing in on her. He was doing the same thing, heading into a meditation, and she knew instinctively there would be little time to act.

Impulsively, she sent out the command firmly. **Let me see.**

And she felt herself careening through that chilling fog that she'd seen surrounding him, careening and landing physically with a kind of thump onto a carpet in front of an astounding bookshelf, one that seemed to stretch across the wall of a very pale room. She straightened up. She was tangibly sitting on the carpet. She didn't know this place, and then her head began to ache with the cascading realization that she did. That first night they were together, he'd brought her here. Here, and she hadn't remembered it until now.

"Well, that was quick."

She heard his voice behind her. She wanted to stand, but everything was still spinning. "Is this real?" she whispered hoarsely.

He walked in front of her, bending over and extending his hand to help her. "Reality, now that's a tricky business."

It felt concrete and physical, but something was off.

"Don't analyze too deeply. Your mind, as it has been trained, isn't quite equipped to process this." He was still standing over her with his hand extended. She hesitated in taking it. He felt oddly cold to her, removed, unlike the night before when they'd been so close.

"Come on," he murmured, and she took his hand, allowing him to briskly pull her to her feet. The contact, palm upon palm, felt like a gush of energy between them, that indefinable spark.

She stood closely in front of him, still grasping his hand. "You seem upset with me."

He shook his head, smiling a little sadly, she thought. "Of course not. I just thought I had more time. You see, I don't want to lose you, Deb."

She swallowed, feeling fear lightly touching the edges of her awareness. "Why would you?" Then she looked around again, sensing the tugging familiarity of this place. "Have I been here before?"

He released her hand and stepped back. "Yes," he said softly. He was just intently watching her now, not a flicker of an emotion crossing his face.

I will see.

It was not a direction from outside but rather a direction from within.

And then suddenly, behind them in the doorway of a connecting room, she could see them, she and Daniel standing several feet away from where they were now. He had just pulled the collar of his shirt down, and she could see it from where she was — a birthmark on his neck, identical to hers but situated differently. Her eyes widened. "What is this?"

"It happened that first night we went out," he stated flatly.

She continued to stare in disbelief, walking closer. "Why, why don't I remember this? And that mark on your neck, I should have seen it last night, but I didn't."

His voice was soft but very deliberate. "I didn't want you to see it. I wanted you to choose to be with me, take me as your lover, and not feel as though you had to."

And then, finally, it impacted, "And this you did by tampering with my memories?"

He breathed in sharply, then said quietly, "I suppose it was too much to hope you'd see things my way." The image of the two of them vanished, and she was left in the great cold room with just one Daniel.

"I don't really like this place," she muttered, still unable to fully process her feelings.

He nodded, "I don't use it very much. Would you rather return to the other house to hash this out?"

"Is that what we're going to do?" she asked shakily.

"It seems so," he said a bit bleakly.

The transition wasn't what she could describe as a smooth one. One moment she was with Daniel in that large, oddly antiseptic room, and the next, she was back on his sunporch, comfortably snuggled up on the wicker loveseat, feeling a little ill at the spinning shift of events. She looked around, expecting to see him poke his head through the door at any moment. But he did not. It remained quiet. She stretched her legs out, steadying them on the floor, finding them a bit sore and cramped, maybe not as comfortable a position as she had previously thought.

In a way, it would be easy enough to interpret what she'd experienced moments before as some sort of a dream. The edges of it had a foggy quality in her memory. She wondered if other people with similar experiences did just that, dismissing them as just a dream or perhaps even an imagination.

Again, her eyes drifted to the doorway leading into the house. It seemed she would have to seek him out. For a moment, she wondered if she should just get her things and leave, take some time apart to — well, what exactly? Sort this out?

She stood up on legs that still felt shaky, trembly, in fact, but she was more than certain it wasn't just the odd contortion that she'd been sitting in. Heading to the doorway, she wasn't exactly sure where he was but remained undaunted, nonetheless.

Daniel didn't return immediately. Instead, he went for a walk on the beach. It was some sort of self-creation that he'd begun practically since he was a child. It was a lovely little stretch of beach that led to a cove where he could sit on the rocks and watch the schools of fish dance around his bare feet. It was usually either early in the morning or approaching dusk, and early autumn or early spring, never the hottest part of the summer.

Here was a lovely little niche that he'd created as a solitary escape until, of course, after his mother had left, when his uncle rooted him out here. And today, he was not alone, as his mother silently walked alongside him.

"I don't really need company," he murmured.

"I'm sure you don't think you do."

It angered him. The whole thing, the whole mess, angered him, and right now, his long-absent mother was angering him.

"I am sorry," she said.

"Sorry, for what exactly?"

"Foremost, I couldn't be the kind of mother you needed, who would fix you snacks and take care of you when you were sick."

"We've been over this before. I've made peace with it."

"But have you forgiven me for it?"

"Of course," he said, wondering if that was true. Perhaps forgiveness was not simply done but had to be revisited now and again like a booster shot.

"And I am sorry about Deborah."

Now this one sliced at him like a knife. "I thought I had more time, more time to fix this. I don't know if she will understand."

"Or forgive you?"

"Or forgive me," he echoed.

"It's a difficult pill to seek forgiveness. I should know. But if you want my advice."

He waited, but there was no elaboration. He was going to have to ask for it. "Yes, please. What is your advice?"

They'd stopped walking, and the warm saltwater lapped around his bare ankles. Because in this little niche, he would always be walking barefoot. He liked the feel of the wet sand. "Tell her the truth. Tell what you did and why you did it. And tell her how you feel about her."

It wasn't exactly what he wanted to hear. The truth often was not such a welcome thing. "I don't know if she's ready for that."

"No one's ever ready, my dearest one."

The bungalow house was relatively small but winding in nature. She found Daniel's study just past his room where they'd spent the night before, but on the other end of the house from the guest room he'd designated for her. Deborah recognized the room from the vision she'd experienced not so long ago. He was there, sitting behind the pine-colored desk, his eyes closed. She waited on the threshold for a moment until he stirred. His eyes fluttered open, and he focused on her.

"Where were you?" she asked.

"Actually, I was walking on a beach with my mother."

"Your mother? I thought she had died," suddenly realizing that he'd never said that explicitly.

"No, she lives out in New Mexico, in a sort of commune of people who find life in the flesh nearly intolerable. I only communicate with her on spiritual planes."

"Oh," she said haltingly, swallowing on a dry throat, "well, that's different."

"She recommended I tell you the truth. Would you rather get it in smaller doses?" He hesitated, continuing to look at her intently, "Just a question, are you coming inside?" he said flatly.

She breathed in sharply. She remembered she was supposed to be angry with him for ostensibly lying to her, but he was making it difficult. "I haven't really decided. I was thinking of going home."

He nodded slowly, looking more than a bit deflated. "I see. Will you give me a chance to talk you out of it?"

"That depends on how you intend to do it."

Then there was a slight flicker of a smile across his lips, and she wondered dismally what exactly she'd said to amuse him. "Just talking, I assure you. No more manipulation of memories."

"Is that what you did? Manipulated my mem—"

"A little, just that first night, first date, you haven't completely retrieved it yet, but it sort of went off the rails. And I thought it was important I get a bit of a do-over."

She stood her ground at the entrance of the room. At some time during the conversation, she'd decided to stay put. It was a good vantage point if she wanted to bolt at any moment. "And why exactly did you feel you needed a do-over?"

He straightened up in his chair and leaned over the desk placing his palms face down. "I'm sorry. I wasn't clear if you wanted your truth in smaller morsels or are we going for broke?"

"You're very sarcastic for such a moment," she snapped impulsively.

"Sorry, it's my nature, probably a bit of a defense," he said a bit hesitantly.

"Why?" Then she felt her throat clog up with emotion. Damn it, why couldn't she be as calm and removed as he appeared to be? "Why would you need to be defensive with me?"

His eyes opened widely as though astonished by her question. "Because you're about to flee out my front door and disappear from my life Deborah. That's a scenario that, at this moment, I can't begin to fathom how to deal with."

What he said absolutely knocked the breath out of her. He had this ability to reach right inside of her as no one had ever done before. "Please, Daniel, just explain things to me."

He stood up from behind his desk, startling her a bit. Instinctively, she took a step back.

"You can't possibly begin to believe you have anything to fear from me."

It was overwhelming, all of it. She felt so dangerously emotional. "I don't know what I think. I—I don't understand."

He walked around the desk and stopped several feet in front of her. "Deborah, unfortunately, I don't believe the problem is that you don't understand. I think the problem is that you do."

She breathed in deeply, strangely feeling as though she couldn't get enough air. "I saw that mark on your neck. It's like the one I have."

"Not exactly, Deb. Mirror images, opposites, yin, and yang."

"My aunt told me it was rare, and I would have to live differently. And that there was someone very particular out there for me that I may or may not meet." He reached out and softly brushed her cheek with his fingertips. "I thought she was crazy. I mean eccentric. That all of it was some fairy tale, she made up in her head to make me feel —"

"Feel what, Deborah?" he asked a little huskily.

"To make me feel special," she whispered, her throat clogged with pent-up emotion.

His dark eyes widened, "You are special, extraordinarily special. And I'm afraid I have to tell you your Aunt Gena wasn't crazy. She may have underprepared you a bit, but certainly not crazy."

"What are you saying?"

"I knew who you were before we met, before the gallery. And I knew we would become companions, lovers, and much more."

She shook her head, "Daniel, how can—"

And then he was kissing her again, pulling her firmly and fluidly into his arms and kissing her. She felt the need inside her rage up like a bolt of lightning. This connection of theirs, there was no denying it. But everything else, everything else that made this seem so impossible just swirled away from her.

"Is this how things are supposed to be?"

It was the playground again, near Aunt Gena's house. It was odd that it was difficult for her to say, "My House." She still felt like a squatter there. It wasn't hers. She was holding it temporarily, but it wasn't really hers.

She heard the wings fluttering, but she pushed them aside, trying to focus on all the questions that were surging around in her head.

"How can I take hold of things?"

Sometimes there isn't any time for all that. All you can do is surrender to what is happening.

They were all about her, the crows again. She remembered them from her dreams, from Daniel's condominium that night. But this was different, more intense. They were everywhere, filling up every nook and cranny of the playground. So many more than before, even on the ground, moving and twitching because there was so little space.

"Is this how things are supposed to be?" she repeated, primarily to herself. "Why are there so many of them now?"

The low ones, there are too many of them pushing through. They're making their move. They want dominion.

Her vision refocused on the playground, but it was empty now, barren. She heard the rustling, an invisible rustling, and then a glow covering everywhere, a sickening red glow spreading over just everything.

Her eyes opened, and she sat up abruptly in Daniel's bed, filled with an inexplicable sort of horror, breathing in deeply in a panic. She felt his arms go around her. "What's the matter, Deborah?" he said, pulling her back against his bare chest.

It hurt to breathe, to inhale. And her body felt like pain everywhere, as though she had passed through something toxic. His hands moved over her skin softly, and he murmured. "You've been drained of energy. What did you see?"

She was trembling, but he was helping, his touch. "I—I don't know. Something bad, very bad, is here now."

He pulled her closer to him, soothing her, and she remembered the question she had in her mind.

"Is this how things are supposed to be?"

The only answer was acceptance now. Accepting what is was the only way to move forward.

Finis

Gravier's Bookshop

A New Orleans Paranormal Mystery (#1)

6 x 9 Softcover 190 pages

ISBN 978-1-61342-288-5

Max Gravier had no intention of becoming a recluse, but after his wife's death it seems his life is heading in that direction. He spends his time running Gravier's Bookshop on Magazine Street and occasionally on the quiet helps the police solve a crime with his psychic sensitivities. That is until he answers Caroline's call, a cry for help, out of his dreams that draws him into a fierce battle for a young woman's soul.

In this first installment of The New Orleans Paranormal Mystery series, Caroline Breslin, an amazingly gifted empath, is determined to strike out on her own and has moved out from the protection of her family home. All is going extremely well until of course she comes under siege from a devastating supernatural attack. The last thing Caroline wants is to run back to her family for help, even though she is painfully in over her head. What she really needs is a knight in shining armor or maybe just that guy that keeps haunting her dreams.

The Hotel Mandolin (#2)

A New Orleans Paranormal Mystery

6 x 9 Softcover 138 pages

ISBN 978-1-61342-290-8

Peril is wrapped up in the most enticing of disguises, in The Hotel Mandolin, the second installment of The New Orleans Paranormal Mystery series. It's opulent, it's classic, and it's one of the most renowned hotels nestled deep in New Orleans' famous business district, but something is amiss at The Hotel Mandolin. PI Peter Norfleet is calling out the big guns to help him investigate a recent suicide at the famous establishment — his good friend Max Gravier, a formidable psychic, and his girlfriend Caroline Breslin, a talented empath. But none of them can seem to scratch the surface of this puzzle, no one except Cassie Breslin, Caroline's clairvoyant mother, who has somehow tapped into an unexpected connection with a tragic ghost from the turn of the century. And the more she uncovers the more dangerous and malevolent the mystery becomes.

The House at Pritchard Place (#3)

A New Orleans Paranormal Mystery

6 x 9 Softcover 170 pages

ISBN 978-1-61342-292-2

Nothing is really wrong with the old Warrick House on Dante St. except that there most certainly is. Nothing is exactly wrong with its new mysterious owner except that Elise is sure that something doesn't add up. In the third installment of The New Orleans Paranormal Mystery series, with the help of the very psychic Breslin clan, Elise is about to embark on a wild rescue mission into another dimension that will land her squarely somewhere she doesn't expect, right back into her past. Right back to a childhood home whose memory still haunts her to this day -- The House at Pritchard Place.

Dragonflies - Journeys into the Paranormal

6 x 9 Softcover 120 pages

ISBN 978-1-88756-072-6

A powerful wizard, love-crossed ghosts, a mysterious dark warrior, and an enigmatic time traveler -- a mystical wordsmith entices you into the world of the paranormal with a collection of inspired stories. Each tale takes the journey of the dragonfly imbued with the momentum and energy of change, following a winding path that ultimately will lead you to find the truth buried beneath perception.

Treading on Borrowed Time

6 x 9 Softcover 198 pages

ISBN 978-1-61342-214-4

For Julia Moreau life seems complicated. Emerging from a failed marriage and managing a lifetime of diabetes, she lives alone in her childhood home where she communicates with the spirit of her Great Aunt Lilia. But Julia doesn't have a clue what complicated is until she is thrust into being the key chess piece in a match between two powerful men of extraordinary abilities on the wild hunt for a mystical creature hidden in the heart of New Orleans' French Quarter. Will Julia lose her soul to the karma of a devastating past life or her heart to the love of a man driven by dark forces? What is clear is that whichever way she turns she is Treading on Borrowed Time.

Appointment With the Unknown:

The Hotel Stories

6 x 9 Softcover 151 pages

ISBN 978-1613423608

A hotel for most represents a normal place, a predictable realm of commonality. One might even go as far to say a safe space, the reliable, where nothing particularly unusual is expected to happen. Or is it? Dimensional traveling, spirit guides, mystical storms, and soul mates separated by time are only a few of the elements dotting this supernatural landscape. Drop into a collection of romantic paranormal stories where that place of commonality is only the threshold, the jumping off point, for extraordinary adventures into the unknown.

A Quiet Moment

6 x 9 Softcover 295 pages

ISBN 978-1-61342-326-4

Jacob Wyss is caught in a rut, in fact on the verge of being engulfed by it. After an excruciating and disillusioning divorce, his life as an artist in a sleepy-college town at the foot of the Appalachian Mountains has become quiet, routine, and maddening in its predictability. One wintry day, his deep restlessness drives him out in precarious conditions to a largely empty bookstore nearly devoid of another living soul, nearly.

Aimee Marston isn't like everyone else. On the surface, she lives a sedate life working as a feature writer for a small local newspaper in addition to several other editorial jobs to help make ends meet. But just beneath, her existence is largely not her own. She is a sensitive, an empathetic psychic, guided by her calling to use her gifts to help others. Unfortunately, as a result, her secretiveness has made her defensive, protective of herself, and prevented her from having much of a life of her own.

A psychic call for help sends Aimee out on a freezing January morning where her destiny and Jacob's collide sending both their lives spiraling onto an unexpected and often disturbing track. Two lonely souls connect, not by accident, but by design. Theirs is the intersection of two spiritual paths, two lovers who must struggle to overcome the phantoms of a past life, as well as the challenges of their own inner demons to carve out an extraordinary future together.

Travels into the Breach - Accounts of a Reclusive Mystic

6 x 9 Softcover 176 pages

ISBN 978-1-61342-323-3

At first glance, his life seems quiet, serene, and even uneventful. Malachi McKellan, a 65 five-year-old widower and author of esoteric books, lives largely as a recluse in a house situated just off the banks of Bayou St. John in New Orleans. But unbeknownst to most, he is also a bit of a detective, a specific kind of detective whose specialty is psychic attacks. Alongside his lifelong companion and spirit guide Simon Tull, a nineteenth century, twenty something English gent, Malachi battles the unseen, and is an unacknowledged hero to the most vulnerable - most of the population who have no idea what is really happening beneath the surface of the world in which they live.

In this collection of adventures, Malachi McKellan and Simon Tull wage war against the most insidious elements of the paranormal. In "The Three," Malachi and Simon come to the aid of a young woman being victimized by a group of dark witches. An old apartment building is the scene of an unimaginable battle against monstrous forces in "The Lost Soul." Malachi and Simon find themselves strategizing against a psychic vampire in "Obsession," and "The Hotel" turns back time to the 1980's where Malachi confronts a demonic spirit. In "Between," a past life is revisited as Malachi attempts to rescue a beloved sister from committing her existence to vengeance, and "The Wedding" takes a personal turn when Malachi must confront painful truths while endeavoring to protect his niece from a potentially devastating union. Travel into the Breach with a pair of paranormal warriors who choose to confront overwhelming forces on a battlefield unsuspected by most.

A Ghost of a Chance

6 x 9 Softcover 174 pages

ISBN 978-1-88756-050-4

Jack Brennan, an ambitious high-powered attorney dies, only to find himself constrained to a peculiar afterlife as an earth-bound spirit trapped in an old Virginia farmhouse with a very much living, reclusive writer of campy vampire novels. Hallie Barkly recovering from a painful and disillusioning divorce has forged a career and exorcised her demons by writing under the pseudonym of Sebastian Winters. Their lives intersect, and two unconventional lovers are brought together under insurmountable circumstances. They must battle an unseen force hell-bent on possessing Hallie's life and bridge death itself to make possible what cannot be - to find a chance.

Explanations

6 x 9 Softcover 82 pages

ISBN 978-1-93493-515-6

In this, her second poetry collection, Evelyn Klebert takes us down the intricate path of a personal journey. Life with its particular struggles, pit- falls, and ultimately triumphs clearly begins to mirror a universal path, the quest for answers that we all ultimately pursue. In this reflective, esoteric collection we can all explore and seek some of life's elemental mysteries and hopefully when all is said and done emerge with some Explanations.

Sanctuary of Echoes

6 x 9 Softcover 338 pages

ISBN 978-1-61342-211-3

Corey Knight was more than convinced that all she could look forward to now was a quiet, reclusive life spent living out the rest of her days in her childhood home on the fringes of New Orleans' French Quarter. But the unexpected specter of her deceased father plunges her into a mad quest for a missing supernatural weapon unearthed long ago. And unfortunately, her only ally is a lost love who she betrayed.

Iain Shaw returns to New Orleans, a city he abandoned a decade before while fleeing a devastating past. Here, he is only confronted by it again in the visage of the woman he once adored — the one he is now determined to get back at any cost.

Follow them both in a wild supernatural tale of discovery and redemption as they confront and unearth the echoes of a buried and unyielding truth that once tore them irreparably apart.

Breaking Through the Pale

6 x 9 Softcover 92 pages

ISBN 978-1-88756-045-0

Breaking Through the Pale is a compelling collection of paranormal short stories by metaphysical author Evelyn Klebert.

"Contact" is the tale of a woman who life is irrevocably altered when she unexpectedly establishes communication with a spiritual guide.

In "A Grey Mourning," a disillusioned man encounters a mysterious being on the foggy streets of New Orleans.

"Dancing on the Threshold" relates the story of a woman who precariously poised between life and death takes a journey that unravels the true nature of her life.

"Isolation" is the story of a woman who inexplicably finds herself alone and disoriented in an old, quaint house on the edge of a forest. Slowly, she must piece together the past that brought her to this place and the mystical implications surrounding her predicament.

The Witches' Own

6 x 9 Softcover 124 pages

ISBN 978-1-61342-058-4

On the surface things seem quiet and serene in the picturesque coastal village of Kilmarnock, Virginia. But something unseen roams its lush forests as the past and present collide and the unthinkable begins to wreak its vengeance. Young Lucy Bonner is executed for witchcraft in the town's distant and brutal past. Her death triggers an unholy chain of events which grasp at the restless heart of novelist Peter McQuade, spurring him towards a quest to uncover the dark and terrifying truth.

The Broken Vow

Vol. I of The Clandestine Exploits of a Werewolf

6 x 9 Softcover 140 pages

ISBN 978-1-61342-133-8

In the heart of every man, there is a history. In the heart of every monster, there is a story. In this first installment of The Clandestine Exploits of a Werewolf, Ethan Garraint is on a vendetta that begins in the heart of the Pyrenees with the fall of Montségur and leads him to the streets of New Orleans nearly five hundred years later. But the person he chases isn't really a man anymore and Ethan has been a werewolf for almost a millennium. With the aid of a gifted seer, he is on a blood hunt that will culminate in a journey that crosses the line between heaven and earth and ends somewhere in between.

The Left Palm

And Other Halloween Tales of the Supernatural

6 x 9 Softcover 104 pages

ISBN 978-1-93493-556-9

Just when all seems well and quiet when all becomes comfortable and predictable then reality bends. Evelyn Klebert takes you to a place where ordinary life fractures into the sphere of the paranormal.

The journey begins with one woman's unstoppable quest for vengeance against a supernatural creature in "Wolves," and continues in an old historical graveyard where a horrifying discovery is uncovered in "Emma Fallon." In "The Soul Shredder" a psychiatrist's unusual patient opens his eyes to a disturbing new view of reality, while in "Wildflowers" a woman strikes up a supernatural friendship with impossible implications. And in "The Left Palm" a fortuneteller in the French Quarter receives a most unexpected and terrifying customer.

Considerations

6 x 9 Softcover 68 pages

ISBN 978-1-88756-062-7

Sometimes the struggle to understand the meaning and complexities of living comes down to a single moment of introspection or a fleeting yet meaningful reflection. This collection of poetry by Evelyn Klebert takes you down a winding path of self-discovery where the resolution may not always be absolute, but the journey is indeed unforgettable. It a wide and varied map of inspired poetry for your examination and consideration.

Visit Evelyn's website at:

www.evelynklebert.com

Cornerstone Book Publishers
www.cornerstonepublishers.com